i

c

o

p

e

TRANSITORY

TOBIAS CARROLL

Thea + Jason —
    Friends! Thank you! I hope that you
enjoy the bizarre stories in this here book.

4-25-16

CONTENTS

WINTER MONTAGE, HOBOKEN STATION

Nathan's talking to me about melancholy songs, about this band from Seattle and how he's getting obsessed with them. His kid brother's girlfriend turned him on to their music when they'd gathered last Christmas, where long drives down crisp winter highways were the rule. "I like it, mostly," he says. "When I've got it on, it makes everything in my life seem like a montage." And suddenly I'm seeing it too: those moments of revelation and realization at the end of television shows and sentimental movies, wordless or with words obviated by a pop song's rise and fall. The people in those movies and those television shows are about fifteen years younger than Nathan and me. They've got good skin and good hair and never have odd bits looking unkempt. They walk wide-eyed in daylight, never squinting because of brightness, eyes never tearing up from the sheer strength of the sun. They have epiphanies and those epiphanies coalesce into something that matters. Montages don't belong to folks in their thirties sitting in a train station bar in Hoboken.

I rode the light rail in from Jersey City at two. Clumps of snow were falling in an unhinged slurry, and had been since the night before. I had some downtime; I was waiting for word back on two freelance projects, and those whose word I awaited had told me they had no desire to stagger through snowbanks and slushpiles. Which was good: it left me feeling less apprehensive about seeing Nathan. Suggested I could arrive early and have a first afternoon beer alone before I knew what awaited me.

Transit always reminds me of transit. The light rail that runs along the Hudson calls back every trip I've ever taken to the Twin Cities–if the cars used on each line aren't the same make, they have to be siblings or kissing cousins or flat-out doppelgängers. Minneapolis makes me think of winter, makes me think of long walks through the same snowbanks that petrify my clients out here. I spent four years there, punctuated by repetition: every six to eight weeks, I would take the light rail from riverside neighborhoods to the airport, would step out into the airport's cavernous station, and would take flight. I almost always returned at night, and sitting at that station, half a dozen standing in random concentrations along the platform, might as well have been heraldry for that time in my life. An inexact isolation, punctuated by a Whitman's Sampler of transportation.

Then I moved back here. I'd hear from Nathan periodically. We'd matriculated at opposite ends of the country; he'd headed east when I went midwest, and he went north when it was my turn to make a return pilgrimage to old haunts. The slender times we saw one another after high school remained close at hand, those moments when shifting and dwindling groups would gather at chain restaurants to update life stories and anecdotal evidence. Nathan generally had a sibling in tow. Having none myself, I stood as my family's lone representative at such functions.

Jokes would be made about the inevitability of things, the one time we talked about our plans for the world when we were twenty-two: the city he chose and the city I chose. The dog-eared rib-jab: you go to the city, you meet someone, you get married, buy the house, move to the suburbs. Have the kids. The inevitability we joked about became reality, and in the years that followed, we realized you could keep tabs on that, fiber-optics bringing us news of last names changed and faces altered, of bright-faced children, of moves and divorces and an evolution I never quite caught.

Nathan had tried his best at these steps, but had gone at them in a grab-bag style. He'd moved north of the city, bought a house there. Some time later, there was a wedding. Two months after that, the marriage dwindled. I tried to imagine Nathan's house, but could never manage it properly: part of a postwar subdivision or something much older; a townhouse of right angles and judgmental points; something older, worn down and in need of restoration. The only time Nathan ever spoke of houses was once, one of the few times in our twenties when visits to our hometown had overlapped. Nathan was drinking well whiskey, no ice, and seemed obsessed with certain makes and models of shelter. Childhood's glow in his eyes, he spoke of geodesic domes, modular houses, minimalist residences six hundred square feet total. He spoke of unnamed places hidden away off a mountain road. The whiskey in him prompted an unusual evangelism, and he began to scrawl figures on a series of napkins, his pen inevitably tearing through each in turn and prompting him to start again.

We kept in fractured touch, missives sent in clusters, periods of exchange in a rapid-fire queue followed by long gaps, a dub rhythm if charted on paper and viewed from a distance. He mentioned that he would be in Hoboken on that particular day, that he would be taking meetings with a lawyer. Later, he suggested we get a drink in the afternoon. Morning of, I heard from him that nothing had changed, that he was still boarding a train near the state border and taking it down. And so the place was set, and as I walk towards it, a bar in a space hidden away, I realize there's no way of knowing what's to come.

I walk from the light rail tracks towards the trains—the bar's beyond—and I look around, look to see if there's a sign of Nathan, if he's had the same idea as me. The schedule looks down at me as I pass, and a few people stand, waiting to become passengers. The waiting room is similarly piebald. I look over at the engines and see cloudlight shining through. Through a gap above, a small rectangle of snow is coming to rest just past the edge of a dormant train. A hundred feet down the line is the bar. There's a dim light inside, sparse grey shapes at a few tables, two at the bar. My hand is pushing on the door, my reflection's briefly seen in the glass, and I'm through. There is no sign of Nathan, and after a momentary monetary exchange, a pint of beer is before me. Through the glass, I see a short parade to one of the tracks; a few minutes later, I see a short exodus from a different space.

The second thing Nathan says to me, after the obligatory hello, is to comment on my head and its lack of hair. Whatever the widow and the monk left over isn't particularly verdant, and after a while I stopped trying to adjust the remnants and opted for the filing down. (My actual explanation of this to Nathan is much more concise.) I offer to buy him a drink and he scans the bourbon behind the bar and cites a name I don't know. It sets me back nine dollars. It is three-fifteen and I am on the day's second beer; we have a corner of the bar to ourselves, and I think it's only fair to follow Nathan's comment about my hair with a question about his lawyer.

He winces. "It's an intellectual property thing," he tells me, "but I probably shouldn't talk about it." The sip he takes of his bourbon is of a scale I'd associate with slide-making in our high school biology class.

"How's upstate?" is greeted with another grimace. I've always thought it strange that New York towns like Nathan's get service from this state's transit. I had a weekend once when I did little but study maps: eyeing bus and train lines, routing them, trying to bring them all together, trying to find the odd spots around me that were inaccessible to all but drivers. Nathan clears his throat.

"When did we first meet?" he asks. "I don't think I can remember a time when I didn't know you." And that's true for me as well. I'm pretty sure I could narrow it down if I tried, think of memories of elementary school classes where Nathan was there and ones where he wasn't, but that starts to back up on the years when memory collapses into a grayness, a sense of a time when I was alive but lacked awareness. Through the doors comes another boarding call and my eyes start to drift. I focus back on Nathan, look at him, envy him just a little for the fact that, for all he's been through, he still looks good, looks five years less than his age.

It starts coming to me, then, this phrase: Boy with

triangle head. Kindergarten or the first grade. We were told to draw ourselves. I don't remember my own scrawls, though I doubt that my skills with pen and paper have improved much since then. But I remember Nathan's: a figure with a triangle for a head, distinct in a series of figures with round and block-shaped heads.

I tell Nathan this and his face sours even more. "Christ, I did that, didn't I?" He takes another wisp of whiskey and lowers the glass and then raises it back to his mouth and takes a normal drink. "Yeah, I did. God, I remember doing that more than I remember most of 1996." This whole time we've been facing the liquor rack, our heads angled in one another's direction rather than looking at each other head-on. Now he turns to face me. "I don't remember shit else from that time, but I remember why I did that. I kept thinking, this has to be different. This one can't be round, this one can't be square. And that left me with a triangle. I had three hairs jutting off the top of it, and I think I colored the face in blue."

Here I start to wonder whether Nathan's legal meeting perhaps involved a spot of drinking. I don't tend to talk childhood unless there's beer in me, and generally a lot of it. And when I do, it's to wake the next morning with needles in my skull and a hard-rain regret, uttering self-directed curses as I maneuver down sidewalks towards food, towards client meetings, towards travel and exercise and passage. I wonder whether this is condescending, whether Nathan will pick up on it. Terseness aside, it's good to see him, but I've given up all hope of directing this conversation, and I've given up on my expectation that it might last more than a drink. These silences are stretching lon-

ger than I'd like, and we're disrupting them with the brief-
est of utterances: gossip we've heard, news of classmates'
childbirths, deconstruction of our old hometown.

After the longest of these silences, Nathan finally
says, "I miss the weird." His whiskey is down to something barely perceptible, but when the bartender moves
to take it, Nathan snaps that he isn't finished yet. He
looks back over at me. "I'm trying to get the weird back."
And that's when he ushers in the yarns about his family,
about his brother, his brother's girlfriend, the montage
rock and a range of familial discontent. He names a bus
route and starts to explain it and I wave him off. "I know
that one," I say. He gives me this weird look through one
squinted eye and I try to think of ways to explain it and
realize I really can't phrase it in a way that'll make anything resembling sense. It's my own weird, and I suspect
inspiring envy is not what I want to do just now.

I can remember how we'd see bus stops when driving
around our old roads. Not the ones I've grown used to
here and elsewhere in the country, with shelters and seats
and posted schedules, but ones that were mounted on steel
frames and left at random by the sides of well-trafficked
avenues. Sometimes you'd see them walking your dogs or
out for a run, transit logos emblazoned on the top with a
route number. Sometimes the ground would have a worn
patch of dirt left there; sometimes the grass would sit un-
disturbed like a graveyard or memorial.

I ask Nathan whether he wants another whiskey. It's
his turn but I suspect he's fence-sitting on the question of
the second round. As I wait for him to come up with an
answer I rub the top of my head and catch a sliver that
isn't exclusively scalp. I've been sloppy with the morn-

ing's routine, and I vow to touch it up when I get home lest some previously unrevealed engagement take shape for the evening. I momentarily think that I should say something to Nathan, invite him for dinner, suggest we go on the town, we two bachelors; that we seek out bars and charm our way through the city. But as the words are beginning to accumulate and configure themselves, Nathan taps the top of his glass and says, "Yeah, the one more. But after that, I ought to go." And he looks at me and meets my eyes and says, "I appreciate it."

I fish in my pocket and find a twenty and hail the bartender, beckoning another round. Nathan taps me on the shoulder and says he needs a bathroom and I tell him his best bet is in the waiting room, two sets of doors to cross. He nods and sets out and I hand the bartender the twenty and wait for change. When he walks back five minutes later, he's humming a song I can't place. I ask him what it is and he stops. "Something that's been on my mind," he says.

He sits me down and explains to me how his brother's girl-friend–Deb, let's say–has left him full-on beguiled. Those long drives shared with the two of them, the conversations that left him satisfied in a way no other interaction had for years on years. This bond he felt he saw between them, and his growing resentment for his younger brother, his growing resentment over some kind of power games and a penchant for putdowns and laughingly delivered denunciations of the See, this is why you're wrong variety. The moments of joy Nathan took from his time in Deb's company and the moments of abrasive horror he was handed when socializing with the two of them.

He says to me, "I think I should tell her something." He looks up at me; his whiskey is half-done and my beer's barely been touched. He says to me, "I'd go just about anywhere for her. Burn any bridge that needed it." He pauses and nods his head and I'd swear it's to the same rhythm he was humming before. And even if I didn't swear, that ten-foot smile he gives to no-one in particular seals it.

And so he looks back up at me. "But it's my brother," he says. "I don't know that I can fuck that up." And here's where I know I'm bound to fall short: I've got no practice where siblings are concerned, no direct knowledge of the genre. Nathan might as well be asking me to do up his tax return or build him a water engine for all that I know of the relations between brothers. I know in that moment that Nathan's got the pull, that he could do anything right now, that he could reach his hand into the maw of his family and see what comes loose or be swallowed by it, or he could return to his unlikely home and blanket himself in isolation.

"What would you do?" he asks me, and all I can say— all I know I can say with any kind of honesty—is that I'm out of my depth, that I was the wrong person to go to for this, that I can't give him any kind of answer he wants. And his eyes shift from earnest to defeat, and he looks back at his whiskey and gets back to the eyedropper sips.

Twenty minutes later, we're both done. We walk through the wood-framed doors and out into the awning. He looks up at the times and says that his train's boarding in four minutes. He gestures over to the machine and says that he needs to get a ticket. Like a parent or a guidance counselor I say, "You know round trip's cheaper," and for a moment he looks at me with hatred and for two more he looks at me with sadness, and I can't meet his eyes.

I cough something out about seeing him around and he swallows something back at me and each of us gives something that's barely a nod. I start to walk towards the light rail to carry me home and I look out at the water. The snow's still falling, hitting the Hudson and turning anonymous. I get the sudden abstract sense that going by train in this weather isn't safe and I turn back around to see if Nathan's still at the machine, if there's time to go back to him and say something better than what I've given so far. When I look back, there's no one left to stand at the machines. There's a blur between train cars, someone stepping on board a train on the far side of the train facing me. Then there's nothing: the snow falling, the trains stilled, the clock tower looming, its face beckoning us all towards home.

THE WENCESLAS MEN

The first time I saw one of them was as a shadow on the gauze curtains of an apartment that wasn't mine.

My lease had expired months earlier, and the work that I'd adopted could be done from anywhere; my default mode was transitory, even when feelings of upheaval didn't actively prompt panicked shudders in the night. And so here I was, alone in a cave of an apartment, watching it for friends whose lengthy honeymoon had evolved into a kind of rambling from nation to nation. I was considering my next move: I'd been living in the same city for six years, and the fact that I bore no affinity for it had left me convinced of my own relative impermanence there.

"Boise," a friend had told me once. "We could buy a skyscraper in Boise for what we pay to live in New York. Why the hell don't we buy a skyscraper in Boise?" And at times, it was tempting: that promise of splendor in another city; the allure of captaincy.

It was winter. Mid-January, to be specific; a time when dried pines still piled curbside. A few stragglers had left electric Santas and snowmen in their windows; down the block, lights remained hanging above one door that played a weather-warped medley of tunes that had once rung out through speakers in the living rooms of my youth. The apartment was on a quiet street that ran parallel to one of the borough's more trafficked avenues. Life outside was quiet, but it was present; I never felt like I wasn't in a city, but neither did I feel drowned out.

Mostly, I would sit in the living room and read and listen to the sounds of the building. I heard water idly rocketing through pipes, footsteps clattering up the stairs, and sometimes light hammering from another floor. The couch and chairs were near enough to the window to hear the occasional sound drifting up a floor from outside: late-night drinkers on their way home, or a lonely car vapor-trailing to its destination. This was a quiet street, where a dog's bark could carry for blocks. When the glare of headlights did appear, they briefly stole across walls and floor and then were gone. My phone barely rang, and no pets called the apartment home. Before long, I had become well-suited to my own sounds.

At ten-thirty one Tuesday night, motion on a curtain caught my eye. I saw a form from the street outside pass across it; I blinked, and by then it had passed. It could have been anything, I told myself, and waited for the room's balance to return.

Two nights later, I saw the first shape with some clarity. Perhaps it was closer to one of the streetlights; perhaps, because I knew to look for it, I was more sensitive to the shadings of light and dark. What I saw moved at a pedestrian's pace; it went past the window at the edge of the living room and then its shadow and its outline were gone. I stood and stared and waited, a book hanging leaflike from my hand. What I had seen, that unlikely outline, was nothing inherently uncanny. A human shape and human motion and human proportions. I would have considered the form to have been that of a passing pedestrian, save that the apartment in which I stood was on the building's second floor.

That night I rested on a chair far from any windows, and slept very little.

I spent most of the following day away from the apart-ment. I bought coffee and books and anything else I believed I might need for a string of late nights. I felt intrigued and paralyzed, dreading and coveting further knowledge of the walker that had passed by the window. By ten o'clock that night, I was sitting in a chair on the far side of the room. My hand shook before it even touched the night's latest cup of coffee. I had stifled the room's stereo and had silenced my phone. I sat and I watched, a sudden student of the way the outside light tricked across and through the curtains' wavering fabric.

For most of the night, I had heard the occasional sound from outside: an owner calling for their pet, a car stereo's leavings booming, then ebbing away into the distance. I told myself that if I saw a similar shape in the window, I would crack the curtains on the follow-ing night. I would seek a better glimpse of that which had cast its absence in my line of sight. That in itself would require another night for preparation. Specifically, I would need to seek some form of defense if that shape proved to be other than neutral; if it noticed me; if it was not simply some illusion caused by streetlights, reflection, and a mundane body in motion.

At ten thirty-three, I saw that telltale second-story walk.

At ten thirty-five, I saw it again. This second shape seemed faster than the first. Four minutes later came a third; after that, the night held no more.

I had once known a man obsessed with political puppetry. In the one instance where my mind sought an explanation for this that did not rely on the uncanny, I remembered him, long after he had left the city for parts north. It could be grandiose puppets, I thought. All of this could simply be puppeteers walking their charges home. The moment I finished the thought, I knew that it had to be wrong. It was the most logical explanation I could think of, and it was comically inaccurate. Whatever it was that moved past the window, it was not a tall caricature returning to storage from a protest or similar action.

On the first night that I left the curtains open, I sat in the same chair as before. Every light in the apartment had been extinguished, and I hoped that I was thoroughly cloaked in shadow. Still, beside me stood a broom with a sturdy handle, along with a long knife I'd pulled from one of my host's kitchen drawers. The mood in which I stared at the play of light on the facade of the building opposite me was somewhere between meditation and a steadily sustained terror; a quality of fear arranged by Morton Feldman. From the street, nothing could be heard.

The only sounds audible in the room came from the watch on my wrist. A glance down at it told me that it was ten twenty-eight when the first of them crossed the window. It moved with a steady gait, and was clearly walking, clearly alive. I stared at it through the open curtains. Its head and chest looked human. A carefully cropped photograph would reveal nothing out of the ordinary; an anonymous man in anonymous clothing. But its arms hung longer than my height, and its impossible legs put its waist about even with the windowsill. My breath hung halted as I watched it pass. Yet something about its motion seemed wearied rather than fearsome. It trudged on, neck never turning. If it was aware of my watching, it gave no sign.

The others of its ilk that passed the window—there were five on that particular night—moved at different speeds. Some, like the first, seemed stagnant. Others used their legs to proceed briskly down the street, like something from a broken psychedelic cartoon. They were all thin; their eyes, from where I sat, looked emptied. I wondered what it would take for those faces to show emotion. I wondered what secret language they spoke, and I dreaded hearing it aloud.

I stared at the window for ten minutes after the last one passed. Ten minutes became fifteen, and fifteen became thirty. Finally, I felt sure that I would see no more of them come pacing past; that if I turned the lights back on and paced the apartment, I would not hear unearthly arms tapping at the window, I would not see an anonymous face with uncanny eyes stare in, its intentions unknown; would not hear glass shatter as anonymous fingers tapped through it and reached in, their faces betraying nothing. None would come this night, I told myself. I sat and listened to winter's sprawling quiet.

In the days that followed, I chose to be away from the streetside room. I'd begun to think of the figures that passed as the Wenceslas Men. I needed something better to think of them as, and that was it. The Wenceslas Men passed like clockwork, it seemed. Once or twice I stood in the apartment's hallway and, unable to help myself, looked towards the street and saw their shadows pass.

And then, after a few days, I returned to the living room, to sit in the blank and quiet night and watch them pass in darkness. And after a few more nights, I crept closer to the curtains. One night, having left them closed, I peeled one back as the last of them passed. I watched them proceed down the street in their own strange strides, walking steadily, not turning a corner, not entering some structure, not vanishing in mid-air.

It had been a week of clear nights. I still had no knowledge of whether rain would stop them or if I would simply see the same shapes walking drenched. Clear nights, I thought, though I had heard less and less from outside. The occasional barking dog had become hushed; the angered owners seemed more sedate. And so I had a routine: to sit and observe the silence, and wait for the Wenceslas Men.

After another week had passed, a glance at the date reminded me that it would soon be time for me to vacate the apartment. My time in this space was finite, and a decision would have to be made. And as I thought about this, I sat in the living room, curtains wide, and knew what my next step had to be.

The next night, I stood on the sidewalk, my back an inch from the building's front wall. I stood as still as I could and waited to watch the march come down the street. The first of them emerged from the din of buildings and low-slung streetlights. He walked slowly towards where I stood huddled and wondering whether I would enter his regard, if he might turn towards me, reach out with inhuman arms, ready to unmake me or collide me with a building's wall or toss me, broken, into a brownstone's backyard.

I had left my broom handle on the other side of the front door, but I also understood that I would never be able to reach for it in time, should such an action occur.

The first Wenceslas Man drew closer. Steam rose from my mouth as I breathed in and out, and when I looked up at his face I was nearly certain that I saw steam coming from his mouth as well. He continued along, never breaking his stride, never gazing at any of his surroundings. He was impassive, unmoved by anything. And eventually he passed out of sight.

And then the rest of them came, some solitary and a handful in groups. Was this more, I wondered, than there had been before? Or was this the last glimmer of something larger: some forgotten cabal or community. Something vanishing, or something quietly being born?

I stood in darkness and watched the unseen passage of the Wenceslas Men. I wondered which of my neighbors had seen them, and I started to look at the buildings across the street, and to my right and my left. It was eleven o'clock; not early, but not horribly late for this neighborhood. And I began to consider the absences around me. The cars that no longer made their way down the street; the dogs that no longer barked; the residents who no longer shouted to silence those dogs. And I saw them: all lights in the apartment windows extinguished, stillness there, stillness in the lobbies and that vestibules. Cars parked on the street with frost unswept from windshields. I stood alone on that street and watched the Wenceslas Men go by.

LAST SCREENING OF "A HOAX CANTATA"

When we watched it, on basement televisions after parents had gone to sleep or on a high school monitor after classes had ended, we were never less than convinced that it had been made locally. The hotel where most of it was set, we believed, looked like a place that had burned down on Route 36 years before. The office park where it opened was the one just north of West Park Avenue. The flat accents of the cast, the anonymity of their surroundings: this was central New Jersey, we were sure of it. Later on, after time and subconscious consideration, it seemed less likely. Those general spaces through which the film's cast moved could have been any motel, any fluorescent-lit office, any strip mall greeting card store. It could have been the state in which I was raised, sure—but it could just as easily have been Oklahoma or Alaska or Wisconsin.

Everything about it seemed truncated: there was a ghost of a note in the opening credits that seemed absent; the title itself—*A Hoax Cantata*—hovered a beat too briefly, the text wavering and elliptical. Maybe that was what first drew us to it: its damage; the unknown names; the fact that it always seemed to exist in a hazy VHS world, a dub of a dub of a dub even in its first generation. None of the

names in the opening credits seemed familiar, from director Eilud Smythe on down. There always seemed to be a
few of us in our high school who watched it: knowledge of
it was passed down from year to year, a generational thing
like some obscure split seven inch.

It was seventy minutes long and claustrophobic and
funny in places and—let's not ignore this—incredibly dirty in
others. That, too, might have been part of the attraction.
A Hoax Cantata was a film obsessed over by, if we were any
indication, a lot of straight guys. There were exceptions,
but by and large, the owners of elusive copies of the film
were always someone's older brother, the guy someone
used to skate with, the classmate who spent most of his
time at the A/V club.

One of the things people were fond of saying about
the film was that it was, in its own way, a kind of cinematic education. And maybe that was it, that was what
we were all looking for. Maybe it was the endless pages
of Xeroxed commentary that we all found so fascinating,
that drew us in, that left us feeling somewhat righteous.
We came for the titillation and stayed for the analysis,
the news of allusions, and the endless conversation. It
pushed us to new places or it simply gave us something
to discuss. Or maybe it was just something weird, something impossible to pin down, something strange that we
could call our own.

Theories abounded and were duly circulated. It borrowed the setting of a mid-century Argentinian story, one
went, translated by the screenwriter into English because
no such translation existed at the time. Or its color pal-
ette was a direct homage to something Italian—*The Leopard*,
maybe, or a Sergio Leone period piece. (Given the way the

color had degraded by the time the tapes got to us, who could be sure?) One theory, all but certainly debunked, was that it had begun its life as a workplace sexual harassment video that had spun wildly out of control. We also heard the whole thing had been improvised. Or that it had been written as a game of exquisite corpse—this was, by the way, how a lot of us learned what exquisite corpse actually was. No one knew. Well, presumably Eilud Smythe knew, but no one had any idea of how to get ahold of him.

In the film, there was a man and a woman in a motel, and they were trapped there. And there was another man, called Norris, and he was half memory and half demon, and the man stuck in the room might as well have been part memory himself, and that was what we watched, him falling apart, him careening into objects trying to get at what was true about himself or whether he was just destined to dissolve in the air and sunlight. The woman was the rational one, the audience surrogate in a world without any space for audience surrogates, using logic to piece together what had happened, piecing together who she was, where they were. Looking for rational answers to irrational questions.

There was an office and an apartment and a strip mall, but they were rarely seen. There was a framing sequence, and there were flashbacks, and other than that there was the motel and nothing else. It was composed mostly of interior shots, featuring dirty fluorescent lights and their all-encompassing hum. Which, one theory went, had actually been dubbed in after the fact. All of the sound had, one commenter had written. And it fit: sometimes mouths didn't quite match words. Though whether that was a failure of process or a failure of technique or a deliberate choice, no one ever quite knew.

The thing was: this looked like a version of home that was both more compelling than our own lives—a weirder, more dangerous version of the landscapes we all knew—and one that was much more mundane. You spend enough time in a room like the one where the two main characters sat, you start to know the intricacies of the place. The weird foam core in the ceiling, the peelable wood patterns on the furniture, the way chairs only bent back so far, the places on the air vents where bendingly hot heat would emanate at regular intervals. You got that from *A Hoax Cantata*. One mimeograph we saw called it "an *Eraserhead* for the office," and that seemed just about right, though few of us had seen *Eraserhead* at the time.

Sometimes I think I dreamt the whole thing. Friends I've met since then didn't have the same cults around it that we did. Most of the Xeroxed theories I'd amassed had been lost in moves over the years; I had a list of the names of some of the cast, but that was all. It gave me something to search, at least, but even that was inconclusive. Mina Patrick, the film's lead, had moved home to Delaware and was now a favorite to win a seat in Congress, I read. Avery Adams, the guy who played the demon? He later foreswore acting, and resurfaced somewhere in Oregon to make evangelical films. Be involved in *A Hoax Cantata* and it would inevitably lead you to politics, some said. Some thought. I thought, anyway.

People had VHS tapes of it, once. And for all that it might have been a local thing, it wasn't simply confined to my hometown; it wasn't something that someone's older brother had made that spread out into a nestled space.

I remember being at a party in Pennsylvania with some folks I knew from punk shows. I was sitting in the dining room drinking a Coke and suffering through a bad sunburn and I looked over towards the television and saw A Hoax Cantata on and drifted over towards the room with the television. I said to someone, "Who put this on?" and they didn't know. And the host didn't know. Someone else had brought it, they told me. And most of the folks watching it didn't know it the way I knew it, though maybe one of them did. Or more than one. Maybe they all knew it and they just weren't mouthing along with half the lines the way I was.

That was a year or two after I graduated from high school. I never had a copy of my own, and so I kept an eye out for it when I was up at college. I'd look for it at video stores that specialized in the obscure, and even in the handful of record stores that had a small section of oversized videotape cases—housing hardcore shows and skate videos—that might've carried it. Sometimes I even asked the people working there; I got a lot of blank stares in return. Mostly, they pointed me in the direction of bootleg Abel Ferrera films and, on one occasion, *Brewster McCloud*.

There came a point when I reached out to a couple of friends of mine who'd shared my enthusiasm for *A Hoax Cantata*. In the case of one, it was the first time we'd spoken in over a decade; for the others, we'd exchanged the usual infrequent emails and social media dispatches at an irregular pace. It seemed strange to begin a message with a reference to *A Hoax Cantata*, but that was how it went. My little interrogations, trying to bring the whole film back through a series of evocations. Short punctuated things based on memories over fifteen years old. It never amounted to much.

Sometimes I wonder where the film's last screening had been. I still scan the websites of obscure film festivals in out-of-the-way reaches of North America in the hopes that I'll find some nod to it, some tribute or homage, or simply an acknowledgement of its existence in the credits of some other filmmaker. Without that, all I have are scenes and shots: a hazy figure moving down a hallway, a tender caress on a carpeted floor, a face turning into a painting yet still emitting words. The more time passes, the more it invades my dreams, and the more my dreams evade it. The right film can colonize you. This one only disappointed me in its own eradication. Nothing ever vanishes, and yet this has. Still I type and search and delve, hoping some evidence of it will return, hoping this increasingly private mania can once again rejoin its natural expanse, hoping memory's promise can be relied upon again.

AIRPORT HOTEL GHOST TOUR

And in certain days, you understood fully where you were at a particular moment. Not here, thought Marco Hodge, and not now. Sometimes he thought of holy places, and sometimes he thought of places that had become sanctified to him over the years. Here, he could only think of ritual and hastily chosen responsibility. On this trip, he had sat in venerable restaurants and watched neighborhoods from the window of a subdued streetcar, the breeze made by motion lending dimension to an idly watched sleeve. In this city, he had briefly found respite from the mourning to come. Now he sat below neon lights. A plate of food, formerly frozen, then flash-fried, faced him. He was one of three patrons; the one seated nearest the entrance, given full view of a room that extended far longer than he would have imagined. Piped in through the speakers above came music, an intellectual's swing. Marco pegged it as something from Donald Fagen's *The Nightfly*. Then he reached down and found a morsel of chicken, weighted it in his hand, and began consumption.

Marco was sitting in the restaurant of his airport hotel. The restaurant of his airport hotel was a Denny's and the airport hotel was in New Orleans, and on some level, this fact coldly mocked him. He would have ordered a beer if they had served beer at this airport hotel Denny's, but if you wanted a beer you had to exit the Denny's and enter some sort of chain bar through a door adjoining the exit. The walls facing the restaurant were glass, and a logo sat sterile on the one beyond. The bar, as far as Marco could tell, held fifteen at most. Marco wondered if the chain bar had regulars. If there were, none were there on this particular night. The bartender was reading something stark and avant-garde. Marco assumed the place was still open. He wondered if their beer selection was actually stunning, if this was some undiscovered gem, if, one day, that bar would be full to capacity, the handiwork of an ambitious beer buyer finally blossoming into relative success.

Marco had worked in restaurants once. It wasn't a world to which he much wanted to return. The same could be said for nearly all his past occupations. It was now nine; ten hours until the time printed on his boarding pass, and the quarter-hour airport shuttle had to be boarded ninety minutes beforehand. His time in the city dwindled. The plate of chicken fingers before him was now reduced to crumbs and the remains of dipping sauce. The Donald Fagen album continued on its way. Marco withdrew his wallet, set twelve dollars on the table before him, and walked to the front door. The glass-walled chain bar got a second look as he went; still deserted, save the bartender. He wondered what might transpire if he walked in. Whole futures passed in that moment, infinite and minute Marco Hodges ebbing away. He could have struck up a friendship or a romance with the bartender; they could have become mortal enemies or secret allies. Possible friends and possible children and possible homes ceased in the blink of an eye. Instead, he met Otto Artur, and that was how he came to take the pilgrim's walk.

At the end of the row of doors that terminated at a soda machine was a set of stairs leading up. The man stood there, dressed in a bespoke suit. He wore glasses with something cylindrical strapped to each side; after a while, Marco realized that these were penlights, their lights long since burnt out. He cleared his throat as Marco approached.

"You're here for the tour?" the man said.

This was the start of something, Marco thought. This was probably not the start of something good. This was an invitation he knew he would accept.

"What's the tour?" Marco answered.

"Ghost tour," said the man. Marco nodded. "It's ten dollars a ticket. My name's Otto. Welcome." Marco handed over two fives, and it began.

The hotel hung low-slung like a truncated letter U. There was a long stretch with two abbreviated wings facing out over an emptied pool, around which yellow caution tape had been half-assedly strung. To Marco, it seemed less a warning than someone's beshat detritus, or a celebration's weather-worn aftermath. From the second floor, it seemed like a giant's grave, waiting to be filled.

The hotel's outline seemed a kind of fortress, designed to obscure the adjacent takeoffs and landings. It seemed to Marco that this had been a failure: though the planes' ascent and descent was cloaked, their sound was not; removed from the accompanying visuals, there was only that sort of terror, the sound of nearby engines and metal, hurtling or falling less than a mile away. The sounds and sensations that this shelter released could only summon sharp anxiety, and catastrophe's illusion. Who needed ghosts, Marco thought. He continued up the stairs, following Otto.

This was his first ghost tour. He had seen signs for them before, on trips varied in their purpose: sometimes vacation, sometimes work, sometimes obligation. In one Scandinavian city, he had seen English-language flyers posted in coffee shops; later in the day, he had seen a lonesome man prowling the square cited on those flyers as the meeting point. He'd stood at the opposite end and watched the man waiting, had tried hard not to betray any interest in the process he offered. Eventually, Marco left. Days and weeks and months later, he found himself wondering whether the tour guide had found takers. Where does a lonesome ghost tour guide go when he's alone? Does he go sit with his charges in haunted structures and wait, a glass of wine in his hand, facing spectral faces? Marco knew that this was sentiment, sentiment he'd pledged to avoid, but still the reservations poked at him.

All those he'd lost, and still: regrets that he hadn't slapped Kronor into the hand of some lonesome man on an August night. Strange.

He had come to think of ghost tour purveyors as a kind of ghost themselves. They haunted, they circulated. The way dogs and their owners came to resemble one another, he thought. He'd been staring out into some ice-strewn sea when an image came to him of ghost tours spotlighting the restless souls of ghost tour guides, who in turn brought ghosts on their own tours of ghosts of an older generation. He thought of that spiral, of that chase, of those circles of failed pursuits. On that afternoon, he had been ten miles from Nuuk, had been leading one group to handle a transaction with another group, had been asked to smooth things out, prevent things from ending in horror. He would succeed, or he would fail. He was starting to fail, he realized. His record, a year before, had been impeccable; now it was besmirched, but not beyond the point of recovery. Hence the break; hence tomorrow's trip, a kind of attempt to affix himself to a loose strand of his own past.

The fucked thing about ghosts, Otto said, was that they never really left. Most of them just settled in one space, tangible, lurking. You'd never take them for transients because of the quality of their attire. They were everywhere if you knew where to look: the man not huddling in a doorway in a rainstorm; the woman in an unblemished summer dress walking in an unlikely season. You could fight a ghost, Otto said, but you'd never win. Sure, you could connect with them, but a bruise or a trickle of blood was out of the question.

They were walking past the crater that passed for a pool. Otto's hand danced across the yellow tape around the pool's perimeter, fingers weaving in and out of it. Marco wondered where he was going, wondered where this might end up. He assumed violence was not in the cards; he assumed it wasn't another variety of conning, either, that this wouldn't end with Otto gesturing at some stranger losing themselves amidst bricks and shadows, saying, "Ghost." Still, questions hung.

"What was the first ghost you saw?" Marco asked. It was something. It resembled small talk. It seemed appropriate.

Otto shook his head. "Couldn't say." He paused; it seemed to Marco that this was a smoker's pause, divorced from a cigarette. "Born to it, or born from it, that'd be me." He indicated the glass doors leading to the hotel's gym, to the front lobby, to the parking lot in front of it facing the airport's access roads. "We should step outside," he said.

As they walked along the side of the airport hotel, Marco wondered if there were rules for ghost tours: templates and handbooks and standards; a global certifying body. He imagined pamphlets advertised in the backs of old comic books and on banner ads that read like religious missives. He remembered ads in the comics of his child-hood that promised x-ray glasses and floating eyes. He remembered his father saying, "That kind of magic's not for the likes of us," and he remembered disappointment from all avenues. He could only imagine what his father might say if he learned of this retreat. "You're too old for it," Marco imagined him saying. "Too jaded for that kind of yoke."

Bring on the magic, Marco thought. Bring on the music and the inevitable dance remix and the mash-up and the lip-dub and the instrumental version and the soundalike version and the muzak version and the ver-sion slowed down eight hundred times over and the ver-sion made as a lullaby for children the world over. And Otto nudged his head into a nod and said, "The hell's a lullaby mean?" Marco said nothing. They turned a cor-ner and were now walking along the back of the hotel, which stretched on. Marco wondered how many rooms the place had; wondered if it was less hotel than compound. A decent man would have asked Otto just where they were headed, would have wondered if this was a yoke and if it was turning into something more. This could be a crime scene, he thought, though he knew his way around those. As they walked, they heard the sound of planes descending and the sound of planes climbing into the air. "Not deafening," said Marco. Otto shook his head. "Not yet."

A few feet down the back wall of the hotel, in a space free from windows, a black brick wall yearned up into the sky. Otto stopped and pointed. "First," he said. "First, there's that."

Marco looked on and saw a field stretching out a few hundred feet towards some truncated one-story buildings. A storage shed or a shrunken strip mall, Marco thought. Scrub grass and a few stunted shrubs shot up from the soil. "The buildings?" Marco asked.

"Not the buildings," Otto said. "Look there." His middle and ring fingers jutted out towards the tallest of the shrubs. For a minute, Marco heard a quietly shattered sobbing before it was drowned out by the sound of another jetliner. The sound, the first sound, had come from somewhere undefined; not the structures, not the shrubs, but a space roughly coinciding with the blank face of the wall. Marco momentarily wondered if Otto was the source of the sobbing. It didn't seem out of the question. When he glanced at Otto, he saw him with his fingers spread out, a kind of shrunken wingspan. Otto appeared enraptured.

As Marco looked at Otto, he felt determined to convey some sense of understanding, to decode whatever language had passed by. Otto nodded after some time.

"Is there a story here?" Marco asked. Otto shook his head. And then he turned, beckoning Marco to follow.

In Miquelon, Marco had met a writer, retired, who spent his days pondering acrostics. He spoke of the structure, said that the structure had to be perfect. Said he dreamt of an acrostic that ran the length of a novel that could also be translated into other languages, the acrostic carried over. Called it a kind of idea; spoke of a schism, spoke of ruination. Marco saw no ruination in the old writer's life: it seemed idyllic enough, if supremely isolated. The writer's house had been full of books, and Marco had wondered how they had come to be there: through transatlantic shipments, or a carefully-chosen network of local antiquarian dealers? Marco wondered if there were ghost tours on Miquelon. He wondered if the writer led them, or if he had been subsumed by the island, if he was now a phenomenon to be witnessed by tourists led along moonlit streets.

As they walked, Marco heard Otto speaking, his head forward. "His debts," Otto said like a mantra. "His debts." It emerged softly, a nervous tic or a thought that was never intended as audible. Marco followed until they reached a driveway: not the spaces offered to the hotel's guests, but a pared-down space for maintenance and delivery vehicles. The blacktop's color drunk up the diffused light from looming poles, and cracks sat underfoot, suggesting an unwelcome age gathered here. And from a few feet ahead, Otto was heard to say something more. "Where his debts were paid," he whispered. "Where his debts were paid?"

"The ghost?" Marco asked, and Otto's invocation ceased. "No," he rattled, and was silent. He beckoned

Marco to keep walking.

Marco imagined the maps and trails that ran through Otto's mind. There were some who could internalize that, who could summon up alternate routes at a moment's notice. And there was the majority, who would dial directions into smartphones and pray that service and battery power lasted the length of their trip. Marco assumed Otto had a story, beyond the age and wear he could read on his face. Were there some songs of hallelujah in his distant history, or a more recent sound of laughter? He tried to imagine Otto in different spaces: street-corner proselytizer or hospice worker. As they walked, Marco felt Otto's logic slowly seep into him, a kind of conscious hypnosis.

Otto stopped and, without turning, lifted a hand towards the brick wall that lay fifteen feet in front of them. Marco could see it: a body's outline traced across mortar, the black line caught in the act of weeping towards the ground. "So she was here, and so she cried," Otto said. "Certain nights, you could hear the weeping if you knew how to hear. Some distant sound. Not tonight. Tonight's incorrect. Tonight was never on the calendar."

"The outline," Marco said. "She left that behind?"

Otto shook his head. "No, that's mine. The Krylon. I wanted an echo of her in her crouch. I filled the space above the sobs. I watched it trace above her, making a rain that never touched. That's the mark," he said.

"Do you know," and here Marco cleared his throat. "Do you know what she was weeping about?"

Otto smiled. "Been weeping a while," he said. "Since long before I came to this city. And since long before I came the time before that."

Marco liked to think that he had a talent for banishing regrets. Still, in isolated moments, they came roaring back at him. It was never the big ones: the grand sins of his adult life, or even the minor transgressions of his young adulthood. These were minor things: awkward conversations he'd had with friends and family as a child before he knew social mores; moments where his own ignorance was revealed. Stupid shit, to put it bluntly. Stupid shit that deserved forgetting. As they walked, echoes of a schoolyard humiliation, of redness in the face and irrational anger, came to walk beside him. Marco felt like swatting it away. He felt chills in odd spots of his skin, felt aches in muscles that hadn't been exercised in weeks. Times like these, he felt himself to be an inevitable goner.

Otto coughed. "Stories," he said. They were walking again. "You were saying something about stories." They were in another parking lot now, one that looked entirely separate from the hotel's parking lot, or the other parking lot of the hotel. The light here was a low diffuse grey, and above them the sky had turned bright with a dense cover of clouds, the streetlights suffused in it like dulled meteors about to impact. The lot was almost empty; all that dwelled there were a few trucks, words stenciled onto their doors. Marco stared and tried his best to read them, but distance and angles rendered the words obscure.

"I think that was you," said Marco. "I'm pretty sure you said they would come." Otto nodded and they continued on, an almost formal procession, the arid night abutting them and pushing them forward towards their destination, a shrine or cathedral calcifying from wind, shrouded by air.

Now they were walking through a neutral space, a

kind of alleyway writ large, maintained in some spaces and heaving and overgrown in others. Vines ran up fences in spots and in others were cleared; rectangles of unimpeded metal that gave a view of nothing: buildings and yards shrouded by the encroaching night. Marco tried as best he could to place them relative to their starting point, but could not; they could have traveled fifteen hundred feet, or they could have walked for miles. He felt deprived and thought of friends lost to time and distance. And then the fence and the vines peeled off out to either side and they stood under the cloud-ridden sky. Otto coughed. To Marco, it sounded like a beckoning. Otto now seemed to be diffusing into the sky; his grey shirt stood in no contrast to the grey buildings and the grey light and the grey sky.

Slowly, Otto resolved. He was standing beside a squat concrete building, a kind of bunker or storage space, suited for small lawnmowers or file boxes of a commune of children who'd learned to ignore the heat. "This is what's last," Otto said. "We part ways after this." Marco wondered where his guide might go. Otto was strange, perhaps insane, but bore no hint of vagrancy. Marco wondered what his home might look like, what strange pictures might adorn the walls.

There was a window on the side of the building that faced them: a grid of bars painted the same color as the wall. Deep inside sat aged glass with wire buried within. Blotches of paint that matched the wall's hue lent it irregularity, both in color and topography.

Otto led Marco down the wall to another wall. In this one was an open archway. It seemed too humble to call it a doorway; less the result of some careful artisan and more something that had been constructed around an emptiness. It gaped wide.

"Flashlight's in there if you reach around to the right," Otto said. "Four feet off the ground." Marco again wondered if he was being set up, if some obscure and malicious plan had been set in motion when he agreed to join Otto on the tour. As he prepared to reach, he anticipated motion, anticipated sensation, something coming into contact with his hand, something that would grasp. And then rationality, some revenant of rationality, took hold and he reached into the dark.

He felt the nail first, rust flaking its surface. Then, his fingers touched a leather loop from which a battered metallic cylinder hung, punctuated with dots of paint. Outside, Otto gave a languorous nod that seemed to extend into space. Call it the humidity, call it a trick of the light, but something about it left Marco queasy. And a phrase entered his mind, an echo of something he certainly didn't remember having ever heard: *ghosts don't live in the light.* He thought: why would they? and switched the flashlight on.

All that there was was grey: from the light through the dust to the corners of the room. The trotting pace of a song fragment lodged in his mind on a broken loop, an unfinished splice. The contours of the room gradually emerged into resolution. He would have expected to see, in a room with this sort of openness, equipment or the traces of vagrants' presence. Not so here. The ageless structure stood before him, its floor covered in dirt or comprised of it. A squall began to stir in the dirt. Marco was motionless as he watched the particles shift through space. It was not footsteps; it was a kind of blurring, less motion than motion's traces, its aftereffects. To Marco, the fall of the dust seemed as though he was watching a scene of collapse; that this space had once held something built, and whatever that had been had been trampled by some looming force. This had housed someone's life's work, and someone else had acted as agent of its ruination. He saw a life stifled; he saw a kind of suffocation.

The dust danced. The dust rose and fell, a rite that rose, and then collapsed to nothing. And Marco stared for five minutes, for ten, waiting for the motion to return. When he turned back to Otto, he saw a neutral look on his guide's face and a green toothpick in his mouth. "That's the end of it," said Otto. "I'll point you where you need to go."

Marco stood and stared and did not speak.

He left Otto there in the field, staring neutrally at the sky, like some kind of scarecrow meant to terrify a celestial invasion. He followed Otto's directions and walked through passageways, tracing a new route back to the hotel that took him through uncharted hedges and uneven terrain. Above him, the trailing sounds of descending airliners had abated. The dark blue of the sky had been rendered darker; soon, Marco knew, the early morning flights would begin, his own among then. Two layovers, a short skip to Hartsfield, and then the overnight to Frankfurt. And then Budapest, and then another drive, and then mourning.

It would be his last trip overseas. This he believed to be true. He pushed his way through jutting plants and wondered how he had come to be here; he thought of isolation, and he thought of potential. He thought of other lives; he thought of peers, and wondered who exactly his peers were. There were those of his age who had opted for families, who now stared at the faces of spouses and children; and there were those who pursued a passion or an invention and had that to hold close. And then there was his chosen vocation, his facilitation, begun as a favor and now something that lent him its own momentum.

He was at the hotel now; he entered the lobby through the glass door and nodded to the night clerk, saying, "Ghost tour" as he walked by. She returned nothing. He continued down the carpeted hallway and passed the fitness center and stepped through another set of glass doors into the courtyard. There, the unused pool and the balconies like squat sentries struck him as a vigil for something colossal and calamitous. His speed increased as he hit the stairs; he trotted up the first flight and sprinted up the second. He wanted out of the air. He wanted some measure of control, and that would only be found in his room or standing idly in the lobby or back in the restaurant, more food before him. But gorging held no appeal, and neither did sleep.

Marco unlocked the room and stepped inside and found the light. On the bed opposite his own were his bag and the other bag. His bag was closed and the other was open, its contents on the table and desk, Marco's own sort of autopsy of another's life. Here he was carrying a half-forgotten acquaintance's mementos halfway across the world as an act of remembrance. Postcards were there, and letters, and books and photographs. All of them gathered from a small house north of here, a town which the acquaintance's cousin called home.

"What'll you do with them?" the cousin had asked

Marco, and Marco had said, "I think I'll throw them into a hole in the earth," and the cousin had nodded and had handed over the bags.

Marco stared at the stacks and the piles and wondered if he could pull that acquaintance, that half-remembered face, out from them. Could a tour of this life be assembled from these fragments? Photographs and cards and handwriting; fragments of a moment in a life, for all that that was worth.

Slowly, he gathered together his things. He would check out now. He would see through the night at the airport. He would prepare himself for flights that would consume books, the slow twitch of idle muscles. He would stand in silence for hours or days, and the quiet would come.

A RECORD CALLED "AMERICAN WOODWORKING"

In Birmingham, Dorman's phone was screaming.

In Queens, I'm conversing with Avery. He says, didn't we visit the Jazz Age together? I nod, his necessary affirmation. I say, we visited the Jazz Age together. Flapper girls and ragtime and powdered drugs. Avery winces. Sorry, I say. No powdered drugs. A sort of lemon spritzer instead. Okay. Avery nods, his drift over. We're good, I think.

The Jazz Age, he says, and laughs; and I feel better now, no further offense inflicted.

Avery says, William, didn't I tell you about that night? About making things known? Sounds that lose and sounds that got lost?

I nod again. Avery's in a spell, a polymath with whiskey in his system. I've seen him in this mode before, a convocation of memories, suppositions, and third-hand anecdotes serving as case studies and formal evidence. Avery with whiskey in his system is not an unusual occurrence, but tonight's context provided cause for concern. A call from Alison had come to me an hour earlier and I'd taken a car here, not trusting the late-night behavior of the 7 to convey me to this corner of the borough with any sense of immediacy. If I see him, she'd told me, we'll fight. It'll be the end of us. She'd asked me to go over in her stead. That I could understand.

Avery had ceased his drinking by the time I'd arrived. This was a good thing, but knowing Avery I suspect he'd felt sober when he'd stopped. Now the full measure of the drunk was blossoming out, had been doing so since I'd arrived there. He'd set down the bottle and suddenly wondered why his ability to sit had come into question, why laying on his futon was now no different from tumbling. He'd been pacing when I'd arrived, tracing a rectangle along the apartment walls. Upon my arrival, he said that he'd been trying to avoid curves, keep the dizziness away, but that his feet wouldn't walk in straight lines. I poured him a pint glass of water and bade him drink, then poured him another.

Avery has ceased speaking of the Jazz Age. I'm relieved; I was frightened, unsure of where that was leading, if it led anywhere at all. He's seated now; deep breaths, I say. Deep breaths. He says all right and I say all right. He reaches for the remote and triggers the stereo. Massed acoustic guitars and echoplex vocals. I'm familiar with the record, and I have to say it's calming me down and I think it's doing the same to Avery. The rare song with no nostalgic tethers at all. Avery's hand is steadier as he reaches for his water.

Have a drink, William. Bottle's on the shelf. Single-malt. Couple of old straight edge fucks downing a drink.

I tell him he's in no position to imbibe.

He says, no, I've had my share already, and almost laughs. So I give up a smile as well, because why not, really. I stand up and walk to the kitchen and don't take my eyes off Avery. Uncork the bottle and take a glass from his cabinet. Pour it in on the four-count and match it with water. I glance from Avery to the clock and hate myself for being too aware of the time—and then I think that Dorman would've called blasphemy for this, despoiling Highlands whiskey with Croton water. I shake the glass and hope I'm blending it well. Now it's me feeling the need to move, and I haven't let drink cross my lips yet this evening.

I think to myself, almost say, that we should raise our glasses, but we'd done enough of that the week before. The whiskey hits like a blizzard on sweat.

I'm a crap one for grief. About the best you can say about me is that I never say the wrong things. I've heard the wrong things said at wakes, funerals, the restaurant after the memorial, the bar after you hear the news. I say what's expected and do my best not to fuck up the rest. Cryptic deterrents, I'll admit, but functional.

Next to no one had stayed in touch with Dorman, but Avery had. They'd tomcatted every six months or so, their work or leisure synchronously depositing them in identical cities, leaving nights & weekends free to raise icons and raze ceremony in their wake.

Avery powers off the stereo. Headache, he says, and I nod. He takes a half-assed swing at midair.

Drink again, William, he says, his eyelids lulling closed, momentarily and inexplicably wearing a contorted expression, what I can only imagine is Avery's sex face. The imp in me thinks I should take a photograph to remind Avery of this on later days—then I remember why I'm here, why he's there, the rationale for my arrival. My role of restraint, of conveyance—monitor Avery to ensure he doesn't tread in Dorman's wake. And I firmly remind myself that, when sobered, with sunlight on his face, Avery will not seek anything else relating to this night.

I hear a foul rattle coming from Avery's coffee table. It takes a few seconds to hone in on its source: a silver phone, illuminated and shaking on the tabletop. Avery's not noticing it, his eyes loose, staring at the window but not looking at the window. And I think, he's had no trouble looking at me all night. Or the booze, my glass, the door. And the rattle's not something you miss: that irregular vibration on hardwood sounds like an iron lung lost to spasms.

I say, should I get it? Avery waves me off, shakes his head, his head seemingly weightier now than it had been a moment earlier. Avery with a brick atop his neck. I glance down at the phone and see that the ID bears Alison's name. You're there, and we're all there. I wish he'd left the music on; Avery's a void right now, and all that I can hear is my own breathing, my heartbeat suddenly echoing through my neck. The call ends and I give Avery a look. He's still eyeing the window, tallying scratches on the glass. I wonder how to get a reaction from him, how cohesive his thoughts are. Cohesive enough, I think. She's checking in on you, I say. Yeah, he says; I can't talk to her right now. I figured, I say.

On his last night, Dorman had paid many a bar a visit, Avery had told me. From bar to bar, shots & beer and whatever else was made available. Avery had done the forensics at the wake while I'd been drinking and trying to call up memories of late-night drives, highway before the interstate, the clamor of guitars and a record called "American Woodworking".

Avery says, phones always sound like pain. About the last thing I remember was, he says, we were outside this bar called Speakeasy and we decided to make Dorman's phone ring like a scream. We did and it was great and...we had some beers there and a shot or two and we got tossed. We were calling up screams every minute or so, I think. Joke got old, but not to us. I did the walk back to my hotel and he went off somewhere else; I think. We were already far from sober when we got there. Early morning flight the next day; nothing like flying with a hangover. He was off somewhere else, and that was it.

I feed Avery some water. Dorman had stumbled or had walked onto the highway in some other city, and that led to the central question that none of us asked about, the question for which none of us would have an answer. Avery says, it was that central ugliness. I called him earlier that night and he didn't pick up. Been thinking about it and wondering if that was what pushed him.

The screaming, I say.

He looks up at me. He says, If you were having a bad night, bugfuck and lost, wouldn't that turn it tragic?

And because I hadn't seen Dorman in years, I can't say anything to respond. It's all right, I finally say. It's all right. I see him to bed and call Alison. Should be fine, I say, he's sleeping soundly; with whiskey spirited away in my bag. She thanks me. I walk down the boulevard, considering it all. I check my watch and set my sights on the inevitable bar on the corner, a long way from last call.

YANNICK'S SWISS ARMY

There was a bar and there was a bartender; for Yannick's purposes, that sufficed. In one corner hung a television and on that television the game of soccer could be seen. Yannick wasn't entirely sure what he was watching, save that the teams were English. Burnley, perhaps, or Barnsley. He was never sure. He could never keep track of them when his more Anglophilic friends would cite their games, their triumphs, their relegations. Perhaps it was Burnley versus Barnsley that could be seen on the television in a corner of a nondescript bar at a quarter to nine in the morning.

Yannick had already downed four cups of coffee on the walk over, and he signaled to the bartender for his fifth. He felt pleased with himself for tramping to this part of Queens so early. Health, Yannick told himself. Fine health, followed by the ancient practice of morning drinking. The early-day jitters, and then a stout. On the screen came a commotion: one of the teams had come very close to scoring a goal. The ball had left the foot of a striker and headed towards the net but sailed over the crossbar. Yannick made a sound that was equally ecstatic and pained, the action of someone who could deeply emphasize with the idea of *almost.*

The essential thing, to Yannick's mind, was the concept of the Swiss Army Human. He'd coined this phrase a few years ago during a tirade, and the idea had stayed with him. It was a question of certification: of being a notary and a process server, with the ability to officiate weddings balanced atop it all. "It's like the monks who make beer," he had told a group of friends one night, his arms flailing. "They've found that balance." He remembered childhood trips past a monastery, intrigued by what happened inside. His father had made it seem like the stuff of legends: ancient rituals, centuries-old traditions, and the arcane manufacture of intoxicants.

Six months earlier, he had achieved the Swiss Army Human trifecta: process server and notary and officiant. He had done nothing with any of these. He had yearned. Offers were made, some of them sporadic; out with couples at bars, he'd angled himself just so and said, "I can marry you both. Right here." He hoped it hadn't come off as a desire for a polyamorous liaison. Do it frequently enough, he realized, and it probably would.

As he watched the movement of the teams on the television screen, Yannick began to note certain gaps in his memories of the last eighteen hours. Slowly, words began to return: words and gestures and angles on faces. And by the time Barnsley or Burnley or Hull City or Stoke City scored the game's first goal, Yannick was very certain of one thing: the night before, he had married an awful lot of people.

On certain mornings, Yannick woke from dreams in which he was a child, visiting his grandparents on the outskirts of Quebec City. In these dreams, family photographs had been turned into puzzles, and his grandparents sat silently waiting for him to assemble them. Slowly, ancient members of his family ushered themselves into the room, sat on folding chairs, and began to crack their knuckles. He remembered that sound much more than the fragmented photographs—really, more the idea of family photographs, his subconscious rendering them into something generic. He had told a therapist about this once—had, in fact, dedicated much of a forty-five minute session to putting as much of it into words as he could. Towards the end, he realized he'd spoken so breathlessly that he had left his therapist little room to reply. Yannick looked up and saw his therapist's head angled back. A light snoring filled the room. Yannick learned something in the aftermath of that, a lesson about attention and walking away. He had, apparently, not retained it for long.

A cough came from Yannick's left, and he turned. Sitting there was a man a few years his senior, wearing what appeared to be a homemade Liverpool jersey. "You a Burnley fan, then?" the man asked in an accent as exotic as Bergen County. There was clearly a correct answer to this question, and Yannick was probably not going to say it. "Just a fan of the game," he replied. "Me too," said DIY Liverpool. "Mostly, I'm waiting for the eleven o'clock game. Milton Keyes Dons and Tottenham Hotspur's Under-21 squad. The Roly-Poly Optometrist Derby. It's all that keeps me going."

Yannick nodded. Yannick hoped that this nod would be enough. It seemed to be, and then his neighbor cleared his throat again. "You probably get this a lot, but—has anyone ever told you that, for a young guy, you look a lot like Picasso when he was old?"

Now there was the waiting, and the attempts to watch the game, and the certainty that DIY Liverpool was periodically eyeing him, looking for further evidence of his Picassogängerdom. Beside one of Yannick's hands was a coffee, and beside the other sat a breakfast stout. Beside the stout sat his cellphone, and he knew the vibration that would indicate a call—some call, any call—was imminent. His neighbor nodded again. "Picasso, but hairier."

The bartender looked at Yannick. "It's true." Yannick was unsure if this was something in which he should take pride. He looked down at his phone, then to his beer, and took a drink. Memories trickled in, first blurs and then a proper scene. He remembered the night before, of standing besides couples and speaking with the solemnity of an eighth grader in the school play. A phrase came out of the ether: *"I'm the monsignor now!"* The muscles of his face remembered a grin accompanying that, and regrets kicked in like postpunk drums. Yannick had another sip of beer and thought of Quebec.

He remembered childhood trips there, climbing walls and failing to climb and falling on the ground. The drive up from Maryland: the question, asked three times over five years, of whether the cherry-red sedan would survive the trip. He remembered encounters with angry mechanics and landmarks and the monastery, the legends of their beer and their cider. "When you're twenty-one, Yannick," his parents had said. As far as he knew, he'd never tried any beverage made by the monks; perhaps he would soon. He looked back up at the game and saw a team celebrating. He watched jersey-clad bodies ecstatic and despairing, and felt a vibration from his phone.

At first, the message from his friend Harold was cryptic: "*You didn't mail the license, did you?*"

With some clarity, it came to him: had he backdated marriage licenses? Did the Swiss Army Human concept also involve forgery? Cue a memory of drizzle, of him opening a blue mailbox's maw. Paperwork in envelopes adorned with deli-bought stamps were thrown in. He remembered shouting and a feeling of elation. "Behold! Behold the miracle of love, you mailbox!" He remembered a voice from the building's third story shouting about the noise, and then he remembered running. After a few minutes, he sent back a single word to Harold, and that word was "Sorry." If it's all in lower case, he reasoned, it'll look more apologetic. Yannick realized that more of these messages would soon arrive.

At two p.m., the first of the asshole texts arrived. Over the course of the next ninety minutes they piled up, some featuring just the single word and some channeling a baroque approach to profanity. Yannick felt cornered, terrified. His friends were, after all, aware of where he lived. They did not know of this bar's existence, however. Eventually, a shout of "Last call!" would erupt from the bar, or lights would be turned on and chairs inverted atop tables. But Yannick was still at least ten hours away from that. He began to think, to rifle through the tenets of Swiss Army Humanity. Could he, perhaps, serve all of his newly-married friends with divorce papers? Would that be too ornate? Would he be struck in the jaw, from several angles and several fists? Yes, thought Yannick; yes, if I do that, I will be deservedly punched. He waved at the bartender. "Is there something that you have there that could clear my head a little?"

"Pills," said the bartender. "I've got a whole mess of pills over here, young Picasso."

"Is there more coffee?"

"God, no," said the bartender. "We stop serving that at noon. Closest thing we have now is some shandy, left over from the summer. It's in cans. We can do two for one; they're aged now. Who knows what that does to a shandy."

Yannick handed over some money and two canned shandies were set before him. The bright primary colors of their packaging loomed awkwardly. His phone buzzed with another text. This one had a few choice *assholes* and a thumbs-down icon and images of fire to round out the character limit. He glanced up at one of the televisions and saw that an unfamiliar sport was playing; Eastern Orthodox Hurling, perhaps. The score was 51 to 4, which was either terrible or historically terrible. He couldn't decide which side he identified with more. He was almost certain that he heard two "Picasso"s in a conversation further down the bar.

His parents had been critical of his Swiss Army aspirations. "There are plenty of priests who can handle the marrying duties," his father said. His mother reminded him of the monasteries they'd passed as a child. Once, they had seen robed monks in the cold, harvesting for what Yannick later learned was a particularly well-regarded ice cider. The monks had all seemed impossibly old; with gloved hands and cowled faces, they silently plucked apples from trees. "Don't stare at the druids," his brother had whispered. Yannick had continued to stare.

At half past seven, Yannick received confirmation that his friends, or former friends, or former and future friends, had arrived at his apartment and were mulling around on the sidewalk. *Do you know where we are, Yannick?* one such message read. *We will sleep in shifts. We have brought blunt instruments.* Yannick's own abilities seemed to have failed him. He had set certain actions into motion that could not be undone without at least the help of a marginally competent attorney. Of course he wanted to send back texted *sorry*s to all of them. And some part of him wanted to return home, to take his almost certainly literal lumps, and to see what might come next.

Instead, he ordered whiskey. Perhaps it would trigger some inspiration. Ideas and memories and a heightened sense of time ran through him. He felt something like purpose. He began to chart a route: further tramping back through this neighborhood, and a ride on the nearest subway. There would surely be somewhere near his destination that sold sandwiches and carbonated beverages. And so he settled up his tab and made his way out into the night, having successfully waited out the day in the confines of the bar. "Farewell, Picasso," they told him. He strode to the subway. He took that line to another line, crossing boroughs and eventually he ended up at the bus terminal, where food and drink and an array of magazines and pulp paperbacks were procured. And as he nestled himself in on the bus, he wondered what his dreams might bring.

Three days later, clad in sackcloth, he returned to himself mid-chant. So this was how it had gone, he thought. The monastic life. Vespers, and vows of silence. Which, Yannick realized, one of his fellow monks was about to break. This monk, decades his senior, whispered quietly, "Something I've noticed about you–a resemblance..."

"Picasso," Yannick said. "I get it now." And they walked on down the monastery's hall, back into silence, out of the tactile world.

YOU IN REVERSE

That's how you do it: step and step and step and step again until you're synchronized. First you study the steps in reverse. It isn't simply walking backwards; it's pressure points, it's the way your foot graces the ground and your ankle adjusts and your knees subtly bend. The patterns will come to you in time. You must remember patience. This isn't a feat to be achieved on the first attempt. No one's ever gotten it on their first attempt—not me, not any of the others you or I might have glimpsed unforeseen on some morning's commute, our rush mingling with their relief.

It's best to start on the late-night lines, when crowds are sparse and there are few bodies with which to collide. It's hard to find the empty space that fits you, that you find yourself in, that you were always in.

Practice is essential. It's the motions, first making them seamless, then tricking your body into that backwards flow. It's the moment when your breath catches: I remember the first time the inhale and exhale became exhale and inhale. And exhale and inhale. And exhale and inhale. And my eyes were closed before they opened, that first blink, of darkness revealing bodies' arcane motions, as everyday as the subway's doors opening and closing, as uncanny as a mind in one direction watching motions in another.

Harder still is knowing when to break direction. If you don't time things first, you'll be sunk. Worse than sunk. Know how long it is from your entry point to your earlier entry point. It's a kind of meditation, living in reverse. It can't be sustained over long trips; at least, I know of no one who could pull it off. Running late from Coney Island to Queensboro Plaza? Ready your apologetic call; take your lumps. Attempt that and you'll be lost. The reverse is good for three stops, maybe four—the flow and the break and the recognition. No one's up for more.

You might hear things. Stories of hesitations and seizures and disappearances. Gaps. Absences. Stories that no longer fit; presences that lack names; names that seem familiar yet forgotten. Sometimes you hear talk of mentors who brought them through certain critical steps, who handed off notes or guides, copies of copies of copies. No one knows who the first was to try it. Someone running late, I expect. Someone who absolutely had to be in a certain place at a certain time and fucked it up, and figured out a way to recant themselves through time.

Move yourself in reverse only when it's absolutely necessary. Do it too much and you'll start to recognize the sighs: certain tics; a vague look in the eyes as you say before—once you lose track of which before was the first before, you're nearly done. This isn't something you can ease out of. I knew someone who swore they saw someone shift out of reverse, then wrench, then render to absence. By which I mean that they saw nothing: something unmade, the afterimage of a paradox.

No mentors here. No trips, no tricks; just transit and learned motion. Whose motion was the origin of this? Couldn't say. I learned it on my own. I had to. And I'll keep it. And I'll share it.

Watch your feet. Watch their feet. Watch the angles, watch the motions. Step backwards; guide yourself towards the doorways. Listen for the chime, and for that chime to come again. I'll be on the next train, ten minutes from now, ten minutes before.

AN OLD SONGWRITER'S TRICK

The week Owen left New York was one of sweltering humidity reaching down to enrapture us, swaddle us, leave us all reaching for insufficient comfort. We assumed Owen was alone in the task of loading a truck, of carting boxes and disassembled furniture down flights of stairs and into a double-parked van. It was a week of sweat-stained shirts, of dodging brownouts, of foregone conclusions about the city and about what constituted comfort demolished. Owen was leaving us, and few among us were sad to see him go.

I heard about his solo conveyance after the fact and I had found myself imagining Owen hit by heatstroke, felled by dehydration. I remember changing shirts twice daily, remember pulling an inflatable mattress into my living room in order to sleep closer to the air conditioner. I would have liked to have shown concern for Owen; would have liked to have offered something akin to forgiveness. But the significant strand of forgiveness wasn't mine to offer, and so Owen evaporated onto the open road, bound for the west.

Even now, it wouldn't be fair to Owen to say that his talk

of grants was a cure for insomnia in our social circle. In lost row houses, if a host had thought of an early night, one might pose the question to him: what was your budget for the last one? Did one film really pay for the next? Was it the same patrons and state agencies gracing you from work to work? Owen was always talkative, and had never, in conversation, learned how to summarize. His films? Entirely different, and wonderfully dense: ninety, even eighty minutes, revealing condensed stories rich in detail. One particularly florid critic adjusted an analogy to deem him a cinematic molecular gastronomist: a full meal thickened with Ultratex and swallowed from a shot glass. A trilogy with end credits rolling before the hundred-minute mark.

Late one night, Ken and Eva's window open, their wedding rings still unexpected. Owen pulling vodka and teasing us with hints of his next film. Already written, he said, and shooting in forty days. Cast? we asked. Of course. Ken's hand on Eva's shoulder, idly kneading skin. Owen's eyes adrift as an old jazz record played, floating from the couple shy of necking to isolated cars passing on the boulevard outside. Two trucks, a van, a dozen taxicabs. I was happy to be wallpaper for this one: telephoning in to their interactions, watching body language and private languages and old references overturned like wild cards.

Owen, Eva, me: all of an age. Adjoining collegiate meetings, with myself as fulcrum, and myself as observer as Owen stood bewitched. And me as Owen's confessor over the years that followed: six hours of bourbon and him telling me about how he still thought of her, about how he wanted to say something, that he believed in a kind of destiny, that he had spent too long with expectations of a union with Eva and too little actually accomplishing how he might speak certain words unto her. And me as skeptic, and me as the sometimes brutal realist, the one to look Owen in the eyes and say, it's not as though you've been a monk since the two of you met.

And it was true: even if Owen and Eva were properly star-crossed, each of them had found their own successes in dating. Owen's longest stretch out of college had been with Alyce, who had broken things off to move north in search of composition and chords and a proper tonal space. Eva dated scientists and rock drummers in equal measure. I watched and considered charting the patterns of their paramours, idly wondering what these shapes might become, what that dance might resemble.

Owen's first film had seen release around the time of Ken and Eva's first meeting. We took the train out from Brooklyn to a ninety-seat theater, now shuttered, on East Second Street. Neither Eva's first time seeing it nor mine, but the first outside Owen's own confines. For subsequent films, he withdrew. He would say: *I'd rather you waited. It's like a gift on Christmas morning.* And we nodded, and we waited, feeling somehow less unique, more shuttered.

Owen's pace amazed, and another dance developed: as his films progressed, so too did the bond between Eva and Ken. Cohabitation to engagement to matrimony. Owen joked one night—whiskey-fueled, of course—that his latest film would coincide with the happy couple's first child. (By my own observation, it was not—at least, slender Eva showed no signs of showing, and there had been no announcement from either partner of coming children.)

But what of Ken? I never heard just how he and Eva had met. He had come later, come unexpected one night, shown up at a bar where the rest of us had gathered and had shaken our hands in turn. Ken struck us—this consensus emerging over after-hours beers several nights later—as fundamentally decent, as interesting, someone we would be happy to share drinks with, someone who might bypass the usual awkwardness associated with the newfound significant others of old friends.

A memory of us at nineteen: Eva with fake i.d. and Owen at a close distance; that smitten quality clear to me even then. Or is it all in retrospect? Eighteen months later: getting cheap dinner before seeing a Versus show in the East Village when Owen decided to spill. The end of our matriculation was drawing close. Soon after I'd split with Marie (Queens-born, devoted to architecture) without much closure. I found myself leaning in to Owen, trying to get Owen to prompt me towards action. I wanted that closure, wanted it badly, and I wanted to be moved to attempt something foolhardy, something that might prompt a slap, a full definition of why things had gone wrong, why things had ceased.

We sat across from one another, our barrier a row of cheap Mexican food that we'd come to abandon as we grew older, after Owen went out west for a year and returned bearing knowledge, bearing a sort of authority that allowed for him to lead us—me and Eva and assorted significant others, sometimes three of us and sometimes six, but never less than the one or more than the other—on outings on which Owen pledged to educate us. It was a thrill, that expansion.

Back to college, though—back to the contracted days of erratic GPAs and dry panic. Me and Owen; the restaurant, the anticipation of bitter chiming pop songs. "Well, fuck it—at least you dated someone for a while," he said. And thus, he spilled. Near-misses and one long road trip they'd gone on a year before. "Entirely secular," he said, and continued on. I let it go. And yet: a long drive from Cleveland to Toronto, overlong, a subdued moment when they decided to find a cheap motel for the night. Owen told me he chose the floor and a blanket, citing chivalry; Eva looking at him for a while and then saying *Okay*.

"Well, you couldn't have said anything then," I told him.

"I know," he said, "but still."

This wasn't the only night of awkward pauses the two had shared. Their own particular dance was an elongated number of false starts, misdirected odes, unread signals that had lost their charge. Owen seeing Eva out one night on a date gone horrible awry. Owen himself on a date gone awkward, glimpsing Eva sitting at the bar alone, telling me he suddenly wanted to either draw her in or go to her himself. "This charge," he said. "This charge I feel whenever she's in a room." We talked about it for a while, missed most of the show, closed out the night drunk in a friend's apartment, all of us unconscious by dawn.

The dance went longform in the years after college, Owen's pining interrupted by his own relationships or out of deference to Eva's. But still, his inquiries persisted, even when he was living elsewhere. "How's Eva doing?" easily translatable as "Is Eva single?" or "Has she mentioned me at all? In passing? In certain coded references?" It grew shameless. For someone who could wrangle film crews and funding sources to make his own unexpected cinematic statements, it struck me as bizarre that he'd never been able to speak evenly with her about his own feelings. Then again, perhaps that was a groove worn too deeply, a routine too comfortable for him to extricate himself from. And then came Ken, and smiles and handshakes and hugs at the wedding.

For us, the first film was novelty. Scratch that–Owen's student films had been novelty. The last of them, a horror pastiche in which an undead Karl Marx chased a shrieking Joseph Stalin through the halls of the Kremlin, had put some eyes on Owen, but he had veered unexpectedly from that film's satire and pastiche towards the contemplative, the philosophical, the untethered from tradition. Owen lived in Los Angeles for a little while and then returned back to familiar streets and sidewalks, plans rattling and theories poised to leap from pockets. His script was assembled in short order; a producer found, Rhoda, who would occasionally accompany us on our nights of singles' lamentation.

And then he was gone, away for three weeks deep in New Jersey, shooting his first feature on the sidewalks and in the storefronts of a sparse Shore town in the off-season. Owen always moved quickly. Maybe it was Rhoda who prompted the speed; maybe it was something else. He came back stringy, tapped out: a marathon runner strung out on bad drugs, irritable and tenacious, fond of neverending laps around a circuit of bars, sometimes extending until six or seven in the morning. I was single then; I was his accompanist on long tears and exultant denunciations of popular trends. He would edit at his computer until near collapse, would call; we would restore Owen with whiskey and go forth into the night. And after weeks of this, feature one was done.

Allied was the original title, and *Allied* was how I still thought of it. A surreal revenge film, half dreamt, set on the back roads of a seasonal town. The characters took long walks through shuttered shopping centers, gathered gangs to purposes amoral, built themselves new drugs. Images still call out to me: Owen's lead rising from a mud-filled footpath, eyes bloodshot, looking like something elemental, like something long divorced from humanity. A murder implied simply through a shift in color. One moment of tenderness extended, dissected and rendered transparent.

Owen finished his work and Rhoda began her work again, summoning craftsmen for a new project of Owen's; one that had been nascent during the making of *Allied* but now seemed eager to hasten its birth. It was a delayed spring, a fermata season, and I savored the walkable city. Owen showed me his screenplay one night: a haunted film about the search for a lost jazz musician, titled *Queensbridge*. I told him I'd read it and let it sit. Somewhere during the audition process, Owen met Cooper, and not long after that I met her as well.

The first time I saw Cooper Staros was at the end of a rehearsal day. Owen had called me in the afternoon, suggested that I meet him with some of his cast for drinks afterwards. It was a suggestion to which I was amenable. I waited outside the building in with Owen had rent-

71

ed space: a converted industrial building, gone over to artists' lofts and small offices. Owen emerged ragged; Rhoda, not far behind, looked on the verge of hallucination. The cast looked similarly haggard, shirts askew and hair untethered, as though Owen had been presiding over orgy or ritual rather than recitation from printed scripts. Cooper was one of the last to emerge, and she looked simply austere: hair pulled back neatly, a simple black shirt, a long skirt below. She looked ready for a formal evening, either as participant or observer: the elegance for one and the perception for the other. Her eyes glanced around, taking in everything around her, a dozen snapshots in an instant. She broke from the group, approached me, extended her hand. "You must be Aaron," she said. "I've heard about you." I was, in less than a moment, taken. And I hoped that the tapering spring might never end.

Late nights at bars. Sometimes with Cooper, sometimes with Owen; never with both, Owen citing a reluctance to become the third wheel and us acquiescing. I'd later find that he spent those nights at a wine bar sitting opposite Eva, strictly platonic, in those months before Ken. He told me about it: he would sit there looking at her, Eva's attire casual and Owen aiming for an unlikely restoration, sometimes wearing a shirt bought at a hip vintage shop two doors down. Owen wanting to look fresh, wanting to seem alert, he later said. He told me that it felt like the outline of a date: each of them single, each of them wondering what the other might do.

I told him he was seeing things that didn't exist.

He told me that he wanted to say something to her

some night. *When the time's right,* he said. *I'll know it then,* he said. He wanted to do this before the film started shooting, before he headed into that cloud of longer nights, that dreamstate he alluded to, those weeks when every perception would be devoted to inquiries of his own work.

So say something, I told him. When it feels right, he told me. Fucking tell her then, I said.

It's like we're already in the rhythms of the date, he said. Like I just need to say the right thing to make it real.

Somewhere in there, eventually, Eva met Ken. The new guy she'd begun dating, related across the wine-bar table to Owen. Pale seeping into Owen's face; Owen telling me that he felt the urge to shout, to say something, to make an impractical declaration.

Then why didn't you? I asked him.

The way her face looked, he said. She's happy; I can't argue with that. I shook my head; said that if he was going to do it, he should do it.

She's happy, he said. Shit, he said, and got a particular sort of smile on his face, the kind of look I imagine prison athletes get on ersatz ballfields after hitting a double. This is probably the guy she'll marry.

Two days later, Owen was off shooting *Queensbridge.*

If Cooper wasn't the lead in this film, she was close to it. On the set daily, her work long and exhausting. Some nights I'd try to meet her near set or soundstage. We'd go looking for a bar nearby—a place that approximated a dive without actually being one. Sometimes we lucked out; other nights we'd call a car or hail a cab and end up at her apartment.

Nights gone narcotic, drum-roll talks on the couch. I'd generally be wired, deli coffee in hand as I boarded the subway to meet her. My daytime anxieties clustered: in the long view, that I struck her as somehow unexciting. In the short view, I shuddered that I might yawn in her presence on one of those nights, that my own exhaustion might offend.

On those mornings after, I'd generally wake to Cooper's apartment empty, her call time an hour or so before I was required at work. She never commented on this; only asked me one night, before we slept, to close the windows after waking.

The walls abounded with neatly-framed screen-prints; the curtains that hung in the windows were an aquatic blue. The wind that drifted in that autumn allowed them some quiet motion, and on a handful of mornings I took my coffee and allowed myself to be fascinated by them.

The prints looked artisanal, looked handmade, looked just slightly askew that I found myself wondering who had made them; if I could become their advocate. There were two prevailing styles in the half-dozen that adorned Cooper's apartment. I wondered where she had purchased them; if they had come from New York, if they had been purchased before her move here, conveyed here in moving van or station wagon. I'd always meant to ask Cooper about how she'd arrived here: whether she'd come to the city to act or been beckoned by some other calling.

Not long after that, on one of her off-nights from *Queensbridge*, we went out for dinner with Eva and Ken, and Eva raised the question. An answer flowed; a whole history unknown to me, up until then. Cooper's own narrative, slipstream to mine. Where we–this nucleus of Owen and Eva and me–had taken things for granted, she had not. Cooper had come of age in a seasonal town and in a seasonal economy, and she spoke of that in quiet tones. "I don't think any of you grew up used to lean months," she said in a quiet voice.

The rest of us shook our heads.

"Yeah," she said. "It's a rough sort of thing. But it also helps, learning to live on a little. Helps make the good times last that much longer."

Owen, drunk, leaned in and considered. "I was vegetarian for a while. And, you know, it helps." He pointed at Eva and Ken and me. "These fuckers, they tell me I should eat burgers. And I eat burgers. But I can go without." He looked at us; the sounds of the bar sliding slowly across each of our faces, and his own face suddenly showing regret. His own face resembling that of a child who'd just pissed himself. "I'm sorry," said first to us all and then addressed directly to Cooper. A pause, and then: "I'm going to go." And he stood then, leaving behind money to cover his part of the tab, and walked out of the bar still steady on his feet.

I heard from Cooper that he was on set the following day with no evidence of hangover. "That was the day he looked at things," she told me. "As though he was studying... everything. Faces and surfaces and textiles. Everything else was the same, but–there were pauses in there, like he'd been slowed down a bit."

That was the other thing about Owen's films: after the first, we knew nothing about them until a cut was readied, and sometimes later. "I want you to see them fresh," he told me once. "Not knowing about what I was attempting; not with an eye towards what the ideas were two months ago." And, in conversation, Eva and me: the theory that Owen enjoyed some part of his life for which the bulk of his work wasn't at the center.

Somewhere in there, I'd felt more central. Owen at twenty and me at twenty; him handing me a stack of papers, the burnt-vegetable smell of computer-lab toner on them, later transferred to my thumb and palm. That flash of remembrance, of late nights of critique, typed in white text on a sparse black terminal. Drinking wine with Cooper and Ken and Eva, our conversation moving on to restaurants and transit slowdowns and underused city beaches. That flash, thinking of Owen, wondering what his process was now. Wondering whose opinions were now solicited as he wrote, as he considered projects; wondering how old or new these ideas were: concepts that had occupied space in his mind since college, since his time out west, since his return to this coast.

Another memory—and here I was getting distracted from the conversation before me—of springtime New York, of Owen with a surplus Soviet camera—a Krasnogorsk, finding odd framings and making corners of the city his own. The front door of Under Acme not long after dawn and motorcycles lined up on East Third and a parking lot, half tumbleweeds, its same outline now rising twenty stories above the same sidewalk. Owen's pockets of isolation, and me along for the conversation, coffee-fueled rapid associations, tales of chambered nights and unending parties.

"So these are crime scene photos," I said with a grin,

and Owen's laugh was two blocks long. At laugh's end, a grin gone askew that seemed missing its wink. Owen told me once about his purchase of the wind-up sixteen-millimeter camera; of his plan to trickle in silent footage of cemeteries and shuttered doors, to assemble something of salable size in a way no-one had before. I nodded and offered to help where I could. Instead of a surreal contemplative picture, Owen would bring in his undead Soviet-era comedy nine months later. I wondered later if he'd gone for the uncomfortable laughs in order to reach for depth later. Either way, his rotted Marx and shrieking Stalin was the last screenplay of his I read prior to cameras rolling.

Queensbridge made and submitted to festivals, Owen took about half its cast and a pair of up-and-coming bands and shot a short, a half hour in length. "You making a pilot?" I asked him, and he glimpsed at me, past me, over my shoulder.

"No, I'm not. It's a short film. A short film is all."

Something was different in this one. *Oracles*, Owen called it. The lead of *Queensbridge* reappeared in this as, essentially, a stand-in for Owen, a filmmaker awkwardly mingling with musicians in newly-hip neighborhoods. Owen had shot it covertly, largely with handheld cameras and a minimal crew, sometimes at shows that those bands had been playing. One of the groups had worked with his onetime paramour Alyce and, lo, there one of the bands in *Oracles* confronting the lead about a shared acquaintance. And, seven minutes later, the same band turning on a dime and railing against him.

I'd accompanied Owen to some of the locations

where the film had been set; had seen some of these same shows, had been his confessor. "Those guys?" he'd said, gesturing at the band stopping mid-set to tune. "Made an EP with Alyce a couple of months ago. Weirds me out."

Cooper's role in the film was confined to one scene—a lengthy one in which she chastised the protagonist for a long string of blackout-drunk nights. A shoestring crew shot the scene, Owen later told me, just after dawn in a small Brooklyn park, Cooper's exhortation awakening dormant inebriates on nearby benches. Owen stifled the beginnings of a grin as the story was told.

Once the night's music had ended, Owen and I retired to a nondescript bar, ordered bottled beers, found a booth in which to convene. I looked across at him. He had his recovering face on, skin inching up from sallow and bags below eyes on a slow retreat. His fingers idly plucked at the bottle's rim, and he had made little progress through it. I had just begun to pose a question, my hand taking an interrogative shape, when he excused himself. "Gotta go," and he pointed towards the men's room. I nodded and went back to work on my beer.

He stepped back out a few minutes later and rejoined me.

"What's the next one about?" I asked.

Owen looked at me, then clapped one hand on my shoulder. "It's honest," he said. "It's the most no-bullshit thing I've done. I took a lot from...me with this one." He pulled his hand back, shook his head. "I shouldn't even be talking about it."

It was Cooper who told me the working title. Expressway, she said, and later confided that she believed, then hoped, that Owen might change it. "Like the song," she said that night," and when I told her I didn't know what she meant, she sung it. "Expressway to Your Heart," an obscure hit from an earlier generation, one that hadn't been in the record collections of parents or predecessors.

I remember Cooper looking especially austere during that shoot. Hair pulled back, impeccable. Fourteen-hour days, still alert at the end. Her seventh day, though: exhaustion. Late mornings in bed steady through to the afternoon. Those days, I hoped the smell of noontime coffee would suffice; I cooked eggs and let the scent coat the walls, let it make this unsteady drywall apartment feel like something secure, something stable. "The mountain retreat," Cooper called it once, and I smiled.

Six weeks of shooting, Sundays off. A quartet for most of those afternoons: me and Cooper and Eva and Ken. A quiet bar near their place, and the four of us in a booth near the front, the fading autumn light leaning through windows like an elegy for the year that had been.

Cooper was at the bar and Ken was talking with friends at another booth when Eva leaning in towards me. "Owen was by the apartment a couple of months ago," she said, her voice taut. I thought of implications and felt guts invert, face go pale and cold. I managed only to cough out the word "Like," and Eva shook her head furiously. "No, not like that," she said. "I still don't know what to make of it."

"Was he sober?" was my first thought to make it to words. "Not to say that he's problematic in that area," and she quieted me.

"I don't know," she said. "He was frenetic. He stopped by, said he wanted to talk. And, why not? Not like we haven't talked before. Not like we can't be civil. It was good to see him, honestly—nice to see him in person, outside the rhythms of a group." She looked away for a second, and I knew she was gauging the arrival times of Ken and Cooper.

"It was a mess, basically," Eva said. "Owen walking around the apartment, just talking about memories, things we'd done. This weird rundown of our history. I wanted to tell him—asshole, I know all this! I was there!" What came next wasn't a laugh as much as it was an impression of one, a placeholder invoking some dry-spell take on humor.

"He was throwing out event after event, and just letting them hang there. As though he wanted me to make some conclusion. It felt like a final exam where passing meant you had to fuck your proctor." Again, the half-laugh. I stayed flat, hoping my face looked as empathic as I wanted it to look; hoping against hope that nothing strayed, that a corner of my mouth might not slip into a smile, that I might not misread these gestures implying humor for actual humor, that I might not cast sympathy to the wrong place or ascribe motives or reception incorrectly.

"What happened?" I said. I was unsure of what to expect: I considered the timing and noted that Owen declaring his love was likely but that it was less likely to have been successful. I assumed that Eva was not here to tell me of a tryst, was not here to tell me of the dismantling of her marriage. But I had also seen Eva and Owen be civil, even friendly, in the months since the meeting that Eva now described. I assumed that nothing had been made irreparable; alternately, I considered that I knew less of my closest friends than I'd thought, and a quiet despair settled into my odd spaces.

"He shook it off, I guess," Eva said. "After he talked at me for a couple of hours, we settled into an old rapport and things felt normal again. We talked a little bit about his short film and about his ex out west." Her face looked like mourning. "He said something like, when I'm dating someone, the four of us should find someplace to go for the weekend." She shook her head. "Which I guess would be Ken and me and Owen and some theoretical girlfriend." Her face brightened, and Cooper arrived with drinks in hand. "And that was it," Eva said. Cooper sat beside me and the conversation turned calmer, turned quieter, Cooper's presence stabilizing it and leading it to places with which neither Eva nor I was familiar. The panic flowed slowly from me, and by night's end a sort of equilibrium had returned.

I did see Owen sometimes, nights after the shoot had finished. At one point, Cooper had suggested I see him. "He looks shaky," she told me. "I don't know why. You should buy him a beer." The city was ushering in winter: decorations in shop windows, Manhattan's sidewalks suddenly deeper, harder to walk. Mulled wine listed on bar-wall menus.

Owen on the phone, explaining a postponed night of drink: "We're accelerating. Need to finish this before the cold sets in, before we lose the seasons." Owen sounding frenetic–the voice of someone chased in a nightmare. Later came the context: a shoot arranged over time; scenes of ostensible springtime, and Owen's fears that they might be marred by a stray December snowfall.

"I'm burning the midnight oil, Aaron," he told me, shoulders adrift with that selfsame snow, stepping into a bar in expressway's shadows one night, the hour nearing one. Glances around the space. I stepped out of the booth to get the round; a woodwork canopy, high-backed benches and a table placed a little too low to allow the space to find familiarity. House pints, four dollars apiece, and back to the booth to find Owen gone. Few minutes later, Owen back from the bathroom, hands still wet, easing himself in. A long sigh, then the apology. "You didn't think I'd gone running, did you?" Owen's apologies were never apologies. Half the beer down in the first sip.

"You all right?" I said.

His laugh in response was confident, even stirring. "I'm good," he said. "Seeing how this film is becoming— it's helping me get some things figured out."

"That's good." No real idea what he meant. Owen was drinking faster now, and the pace of our rounds accelerated. Owen's gestures blurred; I remember of what I said, save a few nods of the head and an occasional affirmation. Owen's speech accelerated, certain phrases drifting off from it and lodging themselves in my mind. "Alchemical wedding" was one. "I'm seeing what I can overturn inside my head" was another.

We closed the bar out on a Wednesday night. Parted ways below the BQE, Owen bounding into a car service sedan and me starting the slow walk home, the realization that a shortened night's sleep and a hazy day of work awaited me. I thought about phoning Cooper the following night, to make sure that Owen had been bearable onset, but decided against it. It seemed wiser to not leave Cooper with the impression that I was a bad influence on her director, and so I resolved to sleep early, to stay rested, to allow for better care of all those around me.

Word came that Owen had finished shooting; word came that a rough cut had been readied. I asked him about the title. "I don't have one yet," he said. "Maybe *Motorway*—it's the name of a bar in the film, where a lot of it's set."

All right, I told him.

"It's a weird one, this project. More personal than anything else I've done." Which intrigued me just enough to want to ask Cooper about it. Still I thought back to the agreement we'd made early on, that I not ask her about her work—especially not her work with Owen. Seemed like too much of an overlap—the establishment of one too many connections between worlds.

We'd sat at a bar, getting an afternoon drink, on the day we discussed it. Cooper was flawless, hair neat, her odd precision always present. That might have been the time I'd said that she was cheating on me with acting, and she'd laughed and said, "Something like that," and we'd laughed about it for a long time. "Look, you," she'd said. "I like having this wall between work and not-work." I'd said that I would respect that and I did.

In the end, the title of Owen's third feature was neither *Expressway* nor *Motorway*. He'd kept a similar theme, however—*Transit* was what appeared on the screen in front of us. I was attending something for the crew and cast—there, against Owen's wishes, as Cooper's date.

"I can't physically stop you from being there," said Owen. "But I'd prefer it if you waited." I told him I'd be there.

From about six minutes in, I understood Owen's reticence about my seeing the film. This time through, Cooper played his surrogate—the apartment, the mannerisms, the vocation were all drawn almost directly from Owen's life. To call the effect of watching Cooper channel Owen disconcerting would be an understatement. The title becomes a motif, as Cooper's character conducts most of her scenes in motion: cars and trains and even in the easy rhythms of walking down the sidewalk.

The transpositions were direct. Cooper and Eva—here called Mina—in college, bonding early on. Walks in the park, Cooper introducing Mina to new places, to new geographies. That moment early in their history when it's clear to the audience that Cooper seeks a reciprocity of desire that will never come.

And the long years to come. The parallel romantic partners; Cooper's work in film. A long flash back to their college-era road trip, a tension as they spoke, laying in separate beds, Cooper's eyes open, staring at the city long after Mina's had closed. And at the end, Cooper getting word of Mina's marriage; the question of whether to confess or not hanging in mid-air and, finally, abandoned. Final image: Cooper, filmed with a handheld camera, walking alone, the look on her face ambiguous—possibly cathartic, possibly pained, possibly relived. The cut to a black screen; the display of credits.

Afterwards, I found Owen. He looked at me blankly. I found an isolated spot. "Can I talk for a second?" I asked.

"I think maybe you see why I didn't want you to come," he said.

"Have you talked to Eva about this?"

"No. Not yet."

"Jesus." I wanted to flail, wanted to lash out, wanted to turn one hundred tortured minutes into a shout and fill the room with it. "Do you think she's not going to know? That she won't see it, or that someone else—someone else who knows her, who knows you—isn't going to end up figuring it out?"

He was silent. I'd like to think that he was thinking some of these issues over himself, but I really have no way of knowing that.

"And..." I thought on it some more. Knew I was shouting. "There's something else, too—was it." I pivoted and started again. "Did you cast Cooper because you thought it wouldn't be obvious? Or are you a hell of a lot shallower than I ever took you for?"

Owen cleared his throat. "It's an old songwriters' trick," he said. "Making the he a she, or... the other way." I don't know what he looked like, in that moment.

You forget the bad parts of the movie. In time, what stays with you is what works—and so it was, two years later, eighteen months after Owen packed up and headed for parts west, that I found myself thinking back on moments of Transit and finding that it had found its way into parts of my mind, had, perhaps, worked better than I'd care to admit. Eighteen months later: Eva and Ken, going strong, talking about leaving the city, talking about buying a house, conversations with them now leading to talk of children with a "when" instead of an "if." Eighteen months later: that us of Cooper-and-me having dissipated one day, that reciprocity having seized; all those comfortable places and resonances stricken from my inner maps.

Transit ends unfinished—Cooper walking up to Mina's apartment days before her wedding, wanting to say something, then turning away, that last walk towards a park somewhere in Brooklyn done alone. It seemed a better ending than the wrenching end to Owen and Eva's friendship—with me warning Eva about it in vague terms, then her seeing it, then hearing from her, halfway enraged just in the telling, about her own confrontation with Owen. He left New York a few months after that. We correspond on occasion, but it's social-network pleasantries, nothing deeper.

That's the funny thing that gets me back to watching Transit, the DVD in its case hidden in the bottom of a drawer, like pornography secreted away from the babysitter. You can see Owen in it, and Eva, and later Ken, and other passing acquaintances from college and later. But for all that it feels like memoir, with perfectly poised Cooper replacing wild-haired and wide-eyed Owen, it still leaves me wondering why Owen found no place in it for me.

PARTY ABLE MODEL

"I always cared for you," he told her, one of his hands shaking. Around them: the gallery crowd, festive and clustered; more than half still wanting to speak with her. Her work on the walls: collages, materials jutting into a third dimension; figures entering at canted angles into the spaces she'd made. Even now, as he spoke, some part of her couldn't focus on him, was drawn to the work, to details that rose out and seemed incorrect. Work that felt unready for this space, this occasion. "I don't know if you ever knew," he said. And then, more uncertain, asked to no one: "Did you ever know?"

She thought first about taking his hand. Wasn't sure of the impression that would give. The first time they'd been in the same room in years, and him, waiting, choking on his ghosts. She hesitated; she thought that words might not fit, that a sort of tone, a keening, might be better suited as her response. She watched him. Finally, she choked out an "Are", and halted. His face lost an inch of tension. "You okay?"

"That night," he said. "Ten years ago. You remember? We were going south on 18." She nodded. "You in the passenger seat, me driving; Kevin and Mulhill in the back. They'd passed out five minutes after the show. Eight twenty, light still in the sky. Southbound. I kept watch out of the corner of my eye for heat lightning."

There was a drink in his other hand, she saw. The hazards of the opening: close quarters and insidious inebriation. It had taken him almost an hour to get close enough to talk to her. And over the drink, she saw a color in one of her works that seemed garish and tried not to cringe. "I'd just gotten this record—a quiet one—and I had it on. Speakers shifted to the front of the car we didn't wake the guys in the back. I had it on low, and we talked. You remember?" She nodded again. He let out some more air, and she wondered if the lines on his forehead would fade as the conversation went on. "I liked the way it made me talk. Brought my voice down to something soft, hushed. I liked the way I talked when I talked like that."

She almost said yes, remembering the conversation, the car and the highway.

"I don't know," he said. His words started to bunch. "Somewhere in there I noticed you'd dozed off. I wish I could remember when—I wish I had noticed when that happened. When it moved from us talking to me talking." He stopped. She thought again, was there something she should say? Give her a canvas of a certain size, the proper paints, oils, a handful of tactile materials, a week away from anyone, and she might be able to formulate an answer. And then she thought, not oils. Watercolors. And then, not watercolors. Pencils and a winding sheet of paper. A tapestry in flux, she thought.

He said, "I think maybe I fell in love with you there and realized that it was a lost cause all at the same time."

Still, his hand was shaking. The beer moved to his lips; he took a long drink. New lines in his forehead were born.

Anything she said right now, she knew, would feel false, both to herself and to him. But there was no way to convey this except with words.

He said, "It's good to see you. I'm glad you're back east."

"It's good to see you too," she said. Not quite a smile, but almost. "It's been too long." Not unfriendly.

He said, "I should go. You've got," and swallowed. "People. Masses of people. It's your night." Another swallow. "Sorry to..." He took a step back and let the natural progression of congratulations resume. He took a few more steps and rejoined the larger crowd; the lines between them and the objects on the walls grew thin. Her eyes could only follow him so far.

The image came to her a week later, and she worked long days until she saw it finished; the final work mirroring that paradigm she had first envisioned, and closer to it than anything before. A lone three-dimensional figure, a man in a southbound car; plywood silhouettes in the remaining seats, a quiet song for hushed voices, playing without end.

DULCIMERS PLAYED, STRINGS PLAYED

A year before, Byron had received a letter from Nathan recounting the circumstances of Gordon's death. Along with it were photographs of the event that followed: the ritualized destruction of four half-scale effigies of Byron. One had been drawn and quartered; one, burned; one, dropped from a great height; and one had been given to the local children to crudely dismantle as they best saw fit. In the house in Duluth, Byron had shown the photographs to Alyce. She reviewed them in silence, staring more closely at some than others.

"The fake blood is really good," she said after a while. "They put a lot of work into it." Her expression was bemused, caught somewhere between an artist's admiration for quality craftsmanship and the strange horror of witnessing a three-foot-high representation of her paramour slowly divested of its head and leg, corn syrup birthed onto the sidewalk below. Eventually, she handed the stack back to Byron. "Did they need a permit for any of that?" He shook his head. Alyce walked downstairs to record, and soon enough he heard her music easing through the floorboards, a tainted keyboard and something looped. Byron lit a cigarette and hoped that this would be the time he'd find the place in him where it might resonate. Resonance found nowhere to dwell, and a month later she had left and he was leaving.

January in Asheville, Byron newly returned. First single-digit weather in years, they told him at the airport. Coldest weather the kids could remember. He'd packed little for the trip: a duffel bag, his laptop, a camera. Reached into his pocket for smokes, then remembered that he'd left his last pack at home. All right, he thought, that was that. He'd packed the winter coat he'd had since Duluth, and he felt ready for the cold, though he hadn't anticipated it. Minnesota winter in North Carolina; Duluth cold in Asheville.

Byron had been drifting from place to place for a while now, a small laptop his sole point of connection with the wider world. Guest lecturing and holding periodic discussions with the minimalist composer Henrik Phebes for a long-gestating book on his work. Arbitrarily couch-surfing across academic America. And now, the return to Asheville, to be interviewed in turn by Nathan for his own project: a documentary on the life and times of V. Gordon Robertson, with Byron grudgingly imported as devil's advocate. The main attraction, the naysayer; if not the whistleblower, than at least the man who'd handed over the whistle.

After the weekend ended he would take the train to Baltimore for a week-long consulting project, and then rendezvous with Phebes somewhere in New England. In his brain the timelines and projects began to intersect and intertwine, entering a hazy cacophony, a Terry Riley piece played intermittently. And out of that haze came fear: a precise sense that Gordon's vitriol had prepared Asheville for him even now, had lain pipe bombs and promised bounties as a response to Byron's trespasses. As the hotel came into view, a three-story fork at the base of the downtown's incline, Byron found his heart beating faster, sweat massing on his brow, and so cracked the window, letting in the chill and earning the driver's reprimand.

Byron checked in at the hotel's well-travelled lobby, traversing levelly towards his room. Once settled, his clothing placed into the room's dresser despite his brief stay, he called Nathan to announce his arrival. The call was directed to Nathan's voicemail, and Byron left a message notable only for its terseness until its final moments, at which point he was struck with awareness of his own emotional tone and sought to compensate, volleying out a just-like-old-times reference and a chuckle he hoped might sound upbeat.

As he stepped back outside, he heard a trilling coming from his pocket. Phebes, he saw, was calling him again. Phebes was on the road, alternately paranoid and triumphant, as far as Byron could tell, and Phebes's calls to Byron followed that pattern: low-slung confessions and Nietzschean exultations. Byron spoke as he walked, using his free hand to cover his exposed ear, and began the uphill walk towards the downtown's heart. By the time he had reached a familiar corner and his call with Phebes had ended, the phone had chosen to trill once more; he glanced at the display and saw that it was Nathan.

This was Nathan's great talent: he could call someone buddy and make them understand that he meant it sincerely. It wasn't an accusatory use of the word; neither was it ironic. If you were Nathan's buddy, he let you know it. It had taken Byron four months to understand this, and once that had happened, his glowering resentment of the man became tribute laced with remorse, Byron's own particular burden. Byron heard the roll of Nathan's familiar greeting and smiled; soon enough, he would learn that Nathan was courting. They agreed to meet in forty-five minutes for drinks at a nearby bar.

Once, it had been their local. Byron hardly recognized it, and by the time Nathan strode down the sidewalk towards him, he found himself craving a different venue. He peered through the windows, saw a newfound layout: square tables in precise rows, each with uniform space surrounding it; far from a place where you could get drunk. File under fatal flaws, thought Byron. He looked at Nathan, confusion in his eyes.

Nathan said, "You still want to get a pint here?"

Byron opened his mouth and imitated a smile. His teeth barely showed and he wondered a moment after he did it just how it might look to Nathan. "You know another bar?" Byron asked. "And who does this night find you courting?"

Nathan looked at him. "I have good things to say about Liane's place. She opened it a while back with a couple of partners. Doing pretty well. It's got a good crowd."

Byron said, "Liane going to be there?"

"Later," Nathan said. Byron saw something, a twitch that was almost a smile, and knew before he asked, before Nathan could even think of a response. Later, he realized Nathan probably detected the moment when he gave himself away.

Byron said, "I thought you were meeting the lady you were sweet on later."

And Nathan said, "Exactly."

They walked through the door into Liane's bar and not ten seconds later, Byron felt welcome. The ceiling loomed twenty feet above them, fixtures hanging from beams, their light reflecting off the walls and lending the place a comfortable glow. Two drinks passed, Nathan and Byron conversing in a locked-in rhythm, no anxious calls from Henrik Phebes or blind acolytes of Gordon Robertson rushing the table, no bursts of anger from either man, no resentment, nothing pinning them down, nothing to fear.

Nathan had not mentioned the weekend's interviews to Byron, and Byron was himself loathe to raise the subject. Their conversation began with reminiscing and evolved into the current state of the city, Byron seeking news on more of the places he had frequented during his time here than had been conveyed via Nathan's periodic letters, calls, and dispatches. And so the last few years of Asheville was summoned to the table before them: rises and falls and hidden histories, lives Byron had lost sight of moving to the forefront, old acquaintances trading up aspirations.

Through it all, Liane's rise to prominence was implied but never fundamentally stated, the shifting fortunes of their old comrades sometimes complimented and sometimes contrasted by the bar's innate feeling of home and the steady stream of patrons that surrounded their conversation. And the community. And the investors who had made that community. And, of course,

Gordon Robertson, a presence even now, a foundation, two foundations, a memorial scholarship and a middle school soon to be named in his honor. Rumor held that a local manufacturer of bicycles would soon be issuing the VGR, a state-of-the-art design; in Asheville, it was said, they would soon be ubiquitous.

They had implicitly agreed that Byron should depart prior to Liane's arrival. Nathan figured this would happen at seven-thirty, give or take ten minutes. Byron checked his watch as he and his friend pulled at their beers, the amassing of alcohol in empty stomachs causing their rhythms to catch and unspool. And when his phone issued forth its glib chime, Byron nearly jumped; he silenced the ringer and stood. The time seemed right.

"Nathan," he said, "I should go. I'll see you tomorrow at the space." Nathan nodded and stood and hugged him. Byron turned and walked towards the door hoping and praying Liane wouldn't step through it before he had made it to the sidewalk. The closest parking lot, he thought. Where was it? He reached back for his phone, the call still incoming. Two hundred feet to the right of the bar to park. His hand was on the doorknob now, turning it, he was moving out into the night air, making a cursory glance down to his right. A slim woman made her way towards the bar; turn to the left, he told himself, turn to the left and run. He thought better of it immediately. As he turned, he took the call.

"Are you there?" asked Phebes. Byron waited to answer until he knew his voice would be out of the range of Liane's ears. "Are you there?" A pause, and again: "Are you there?" He heard the sounds of the bar coming through a temporarily opened door and heard them slide shut and said: "I'm here." There would be no reckoning with Liane tonight, and he wondered whether he might be fortunate enough on this trip to avoid that interaction altogether. She had once told him, *I have to stand by family on this*, and it had been their last conversation. Even though she had never been close with Gordon; even though Byron had almost forgotten to consider that connection between Liane and Gordon.

Byron found himself entering a conversational rhythm with Phebes deeply unlike the one in which he had engaged with Nathan, one that peaked and fell, each participant reassuring the other in certain ways and parsing interrogations in others, as Byron conversed with Henrik Phebes while huddled against a corner in a parking lot, it became clear to him that he resembled a fugitive, that he would pull himself smaller if he could, that the passing of headlights and pedestrians made him involuntarily shake, shivers that denied the cold.

Byron understood that the bulk of the weekend would be spent with Nathan, that much of it would be spent in the downtown, that Nathan's home and Nathan's studio and Nathan's preferred bars and restaurants were all found there. And so Byron walked down the hill towards his hotel once more, still seeking the presence of others somewhere other than streets that echoed familiar facades and brought to mind memories of a time before natural impulses had led to a clash. Were he to spend too much time alone, he knew, the old conversations, the rehearsed ones with Gordon and with Liane, the accusations and apologies, would come to the fore.

Forty minutes later, after finding the hotel bar empty,

he walked the corridors of a mall a mile or two from the downtown. Here there was passage, here there was an appropriate density of people. No calls from Phebes since the parking lot, Byron considered, and then remembered that Phebes was performing that evening, that if Phebes did call it would be much later that night.

As Byron passed a wall near the bathrooms, he saw a plaque, a familiar face rising from bronze. Even here, he thought. Byron read "Philanthropist and Hero" below Gordon's name, and wanted to cough, wanted someone to whom he could decry the plaque's language, could reference the work in which he had attempted to render that imagined heroism human. The report, practically his report, now cushioned by lawsuits and effectively suppressed for decades to come; the cause of so many flaws, so much brokenness. That schism that had separated Gordon's friends from his family.

He had traded one identity for another, Byron considered, had exchanged Gordon's lofty patronage for the ebbs and tremors brought by Phebes. He looked back at the plaque, Gordon's face rendered stoic, and shook his own head involuntarily. He stepped outside, the hood of his jacket up, shielded from the cold.

He would call the hotel soon enough, he knew. He would call and have them arrange transportation back. This he knew. He wanted to walk, though, suddenly wanting the solitude, a calm traversal of the outside of the building, his vision reduced, his progress occasionally impeded by streams of shoppers pouring from department store doors like blood into a syringe. He walked on, his gaze locked into what fell immediately before him. He walked and wondered whether his most feverish imaginings might be true: that Gordon had lain a posthumous vengeance before him, had left actions and triggers in place. Byron walked on. No blows fell, no shots came, no angered shouts or sounds of advancing footsteps could be heard. Tomorrow he would memorialize an old friend by rendering him human. For now there was nothing left but to walk into the night with no anchor, his walk the only certainty.

WHY I WAS NOT IN NEW JERSEY FOR

CHRISTMAS IN 1997

If I'm going to be honest, I should probably say that things in my life went awry starting in the second half of 1997. Nothing tragic was involved, but I felt out of my depth, wrestling with a kind of sustained failure that stretched over weeks and months, sometimes receding before just as quickly leaping back into place. I was halfway through college, interning at a film's production office in Soho. Sometimes I'd get drafted to come in on weekends to sign for FedEx deliveries. I'd sit and read Hubert Selby Jr. and wonder if I should stop being straight edge.

The job wrapped up in the third week of December. I was pretty much done with finals by the time I received an email telling me to come down and pick up a crew jacket. This was pretty convenient: the office was south of my dorm, and south of there was a friend's apartment near the Seaport, where I had to drop off a book that I'd been lent. I had a ten-minute walk to get to the office and I figured, why wear a jacket when I'd be getting one when I arrived? And so I was brisk in my walking—so brisk, in fact, that I began sweating. Sweating without a jacket in forty-degree weather; I probably should have gleaned that something was wrong. And then I was in the jacket, and I felt like I was gushing. Sweat ran into my eyes, blurring contact lenses and earning me some stares as I continued on. I figured I'd flush it out of me; it made sense at the time. I got to my friend's apartment, handed off the book, got some more stares, and found my way to the subway. Hello, Broadway-Nassau. Hello, stairways up and down and unclear signage. I spent ten minutes on one platform before I realized it was the wrong one; I found my way down some more stairs, and stepped on board that train when it came. In the initial announcement, it sounded like the conductor was saying it was the E.

I was the only one on the car. I took off my jacket and folded it in my lap and felt the train move. And on we went; no stops were made for the next hour. Finally, I heard the voice of the conductor: "This is the 8 line, making express stops to Los Angeles. Next stop on this train will be Marfa, Texas. Marfa is the next stop." And I thought, fuck this year.

My fever broke somewhere under what I believe to have been Tennessee. Sometimes we would stop; the doors would open, and I would hear the conductor's voice say, "Please return to the train in an hour." And so I'd step onto these platforms under the earth and stretch my legs. There were vending machines there, and shower stalls you could rent, all automated. I'd clean up and feed myself and would get back on the train. My new jacket became my pillow soon enough; it never felt soft. I bought reading material there, most science fiction novels I'd already read in high school.

The 8 express stopped at Marfa; no one got off, and no one got on. The name of the next stop came out garbled, and it was another two days under the earth before we got there. I thought, shit, I don't know anyone in Los Angeles; why wait even longer? Four hours later, we came to the next station, the one with the indistinct name. I stepped out of the train and onto the lonesome platform and looked around. No one else was there, either on the platform or near the turnstiles I stepped through or the steps leading above ground. Here it was hot; here my sweat was sensible. There was a newsstand and a pay phone beside the desert station. I looked at the newspapers and saw that it was January, and that was when it hit me, that I was late for so many things.

WESTERN BRIDGES

A dozen bridges in Portland, and not one meant for him. It was a psychological condition, the doctors had told him; a side effect of the electric shock and blunt trauma, the accident that flung him from his Forest Hills apartment, out of the five boroughs, from one shore to its Janus three thousand miles away. He now felt an uneasiness around elevation, around the passage over water; was hamstrung by newly-risen phobias: the Eastern seaboard and any craft with wheels. The consideration of the Atlantic shoreline pinioned him, as though he was suddenly witness to his insignificance in comparison with it. He would fade for ninety seconds at a time, face pale and eyes sightless; blanks in his perception far worse than the alcoholic blackouts he'd had at a younger age. Always he'd loved the ocean, and now the ocean had turned on him, grown hostile, marshalled its forces to grapple with his sense of place.

As for wheels: he could watch cars without a problem. Bicycles, motorcycles, his cousin's daughter's tricycle: all benign. Step inside a car or a train and panic would overtake him; an intense claustrophobia he felt nowhere else. The mere thought of setting foot inside a plane was enough to make him nauseous. The doctors sought drugs, but none brought him relief; none withdrew the obstacles now entrenched so deeply in his mind's firmament. And so he had walked from the hostile coast to the benign one, keeping pace with the day, feeling as though he'd been shunted into another era where society's nights were absent, where birdcalls and the motion of bats' wings overhead were the backdrop. In those months, he found himself longing for a roadside tavern and a room for the night. He camped, periodically replenishing his supplies. Work had been good for him; insurance's settlement even more so. Checks made out to him, the awkward cadences of a name he'd never liked emblazoned on envelopes: WESTON MARIS.

Minneapolis was where he lingered; he quickened his pace to reach Portland before winter hit. There was a room there in which he could crash for a few months, acquire his bearings, train himself to think only of the new ocean, which he found he could consider without fear of panic. Streetcars, the great unknown. His first night in town, late in November, he'd washed the residue of his trip from his body, shaved, cut the hair on his head to something manageable. The couple whose apartment he would be occupying was in town for a few nights more: old friends of his, they were en route to six months on another continent, paid for by someone's employer. Paid well enough that he could dwell here and not think of employment for a while. Couples surrounded him: those that he'd left in New York and those that were newly leaving him here.

His first full day in Portland, maneuvering through the city's downtown, the steady isolated beat of his long walk replaced by a drum corps, he caught sight of one of the city's bridges in the distance and found irrational nerves causing his blood to race. The concept of crossing the bridge rendered as unthinkable as riding the subway, as hitchhiking through Montana, as sailing from New Haven to Portsmouth.

"I got electrocuted," he told the afternoon bartender. "I was welding something, one piece of wire to another, and it sparked. It made me complicated."

"Welding what?"

"Old keyboards. Back east, I made music."

"You don't anymore?"

"Phobias."

"Phobias because your brain got rewired?"

Weston took a drink. "No. A genuine phobia: that if I press the button to make music again, it'll all repeat itself, and I'll be walking back cross-country through the winter." Another drink, and then a patron caught on, said wait a minute and launched an inquiry into Weston's traversal.

Weston ordered another beer and wondered if he was settling into an identity here: stranded, rambling, the man with a hell of a story to tell. Drinks paid for by a story; that same story, again and again. He could ease into it, he realized. A local. Save himself the trouble of looking for a social circle, for things to do now that he called the northwest home. Stories told to the unemployed and the off-shift guys and the lunchtime restaurant workers. Finding himself at home in a bar with a view of three bridges, face turned away from the windows.

He said, "I need to find a way over one of those

bridges some day." He heard someone else say "What?" from behind him and shook his head. A version of "Will the Circle Be Unbroken" filtered over the bar's speakers; he recognized it immediately, found himself nodding his head to the song's rhythms. Later, the sky long past blue, a handful of beer in his blood, he said to no one in particular, "I should get work out here."

Said someone anonymous: "What're you good at?"

"Walking," said Weston. And half an hour later he was doing exactly that, south—he thought it was south—on 23rd, northwest gone southeast. Not drunk now, but not exactly sober either; walking weather, motion to shield him from the cold. A bridge in the distance; he looked over a new building for it and felt his heart's rush. He wanted there to be someone to whom he could ask the question: is that physical, that quickening just from the beer and the pace; or is it mental, the old irrationality rising up again? There was no one who could answer this save himself, and he was far from infallible. He wanted to sleep; the sidewalks felt like unfamiliar footing beneath his soles, and yet he also wanted to enter a fresh bar and drink until he blurred to a comfortable state. He was close to his friends' dwelling now, he knew. He could sleep; wake the next morning to blue corn pancakes and better coffee than he'd had in half a year.

And so the bar he walked into was quiet. No pool tables or flashing lights or youthspeak clientele. Seated at the bar was a woman quietly reading a comic book called *Phonogram*; two others were hunched over sketchbooks. Winter was at the door. Weston could see this bar in the coming season: parkas and thick fleeces and army surplus greatcoats hung on the wall, mulled wine on the specials board; the beers on tap denser, the laughter fuller, the drinking spells longer; anything to prolong the stay inside, where the cold had no province. Above the bar, a shrine to someone's lost friend. From the jukebox, subdued pop music, catchy, splitting the difference between a backwards look and a backwards glance.

He listened as the song grew; heard a drumbeat that echoed the first he'd ever learned. Behind him: "First snowfall's on for tomorrow, I hear." So he'd arrived in town just in time. The woman with the comic book was asking if anyone had a light; Weston knew someone back east, a nonsmoker, who owned a Zippo for occasions just like this. Weston walked the length of the place after his second drink; saw a bulletin board with the usual arrangement of tearsheet ads, event flyers, and business cards. He saw a flyer up for a used mandolin and tore off one of the accompanying phone numbers.

Back to the bar; another beer with the promise that the next would be comped. He finished it and felt an impulse to walk outside; he found himself going down the street, down to Burnside, his pace faster, a destination at least worth considering. Sweat below his coat, he knew; his shirt's color now mottled with darker patches. Down Burnside, following a trail he'd traced once before, his body falling into an easy pattern. Half an hour later, he stood at the base of a quarter-mile bridge over which he'd been driven years before. The concept of crossing the river wrenched his pace. Memory guided him to the pedestrian path. Two steps. Fear parted enough to allow him some glimpse of how he must look: drunk or otherwise distorted. Fear parted enough to leave him concerned for his safety. He took two more steps; took three more, the Willamette below. Another step, and he realized there was no destination in mind. The first walk he'd taken in a year where that was the case. Bile rushing, his head aching, he continued on.

TWENTY MINUTES' ROAD

Exhale; he sang, exhale. The snow drifting to earth around him, the cryptic American sounds from the front porch, and the patterns and colors below. Exhale.

Geoff Mullen stood below the painting and heard the sound of scraping come through the window. A guttural ratcheting moved into his ears, sounding to Geoff like something low and clawed shuffling its way from the street. It would be years before he'd grow accustomed to this sound, and yet something was dimly familiar about it, echo-not-an-echo, something that reached back to the years when he had no control, the years before he began to understand control itself. He looked to his right and saw the cabinet and suddenly became aware of his hair and remembered his mother's warning, knew suddenly what he had to do, what he had to seek.

The cabinet was stout; once, to Geoff, it had been tall. He still needed both arms to pull the middle drawer out, the one they kept the gloves and scarves and hats in. He planted his feet on the floor, the way his father had taught him, and took a handle in each hand. He pulled and it opened. He took a red cotton cap from within and drew it over his ears. He needed to wait now: he was dressed, had dressed himself for the cold weather for the first time, and now he needed to wait for someone to come downstairs and say that it was okay to go outside. He closed the drawer and looked out the front windows and saw white, stingingly bright, in lumps and planes, a reduction of a view that had begun to feel familiar. Grey and green hovered, tacitly obscured, and further out from the windows was something red in motion. His father, he realized finally, his father clearing the driveway. And so Geoff waited for his mother.

He stood there in his cap and jacket and the boots that it had taken him ten minutes to tug onto his feet and looked up at the painting. His mother had explained it once to him, the story of it, and he'd forgotten. It hung like a window on the wall, even if the colors that lay within its frame looked somehow diminished. Around its edges was a doorway, and the painting was mostly the view through that door: a stream, the side of a mountain. Blue running through green circled by brown. In the center of it, two figures, a man and a woman, red shirt and yellow dress, overlapping.

The red now smudged with age. Green diluted by ash. Yellow and blue faded by chemistry.

It was a little over a foot high, this window of his, further bounded by a silver-edged black frame. Geoff was looking at a cluster of trees, squinting, walking closer and squinting even more, trying to isolate that tiny clutch, searching for that detail to make it more real to him, as real as the trees in back of the school, the trees that he saw when going past the county park. And then a creaking came on the stairs.

The creak came when anyone walked down it, regardless of size. For as long as he'd been walking, even he had triggered the creak. Their cat alone could navigate the stairs silently. Geoff looked up and up and saw his mother making her way down.

"Honey, why are you dressed like that?" she asked.

He beamed at her and said, "I dressed myself, Mom. I dressed to go outside and got my boots on all by myself..." and let his voice trail off as she came to a stop a few feet from him. She had a nervous look of pride on her face and she reached up to move some hair away from her forehead. She still towered over him. He'd beaten the bookcase and the cabinet in the past year, but his mother still won out for height. His mother and the sapling in the back garden, planted when he was four.

She said, "It's too cold right now. I'm sorry, but it's just too cold."

"But Dad's outside."

"Your father's a grown-up. He can handle it."

His cheeks were starting to get hot. "But I'm dressed for it!"

"I'm sorry. It's ten degrees out right now, and I don't want you to get frostbite. If it warms up later you can go."

His voice crackled, lost its dignity. "But I want to go now!"

She took a deep breath and fixed her eyes on him and said, "Don't shout". And he knew that look in her eyes, knew that it was the lead-in for a look that could make him cry even if she began to flash it at him, and didn't say anything. "You can watch TV if you want. School's closed today."

He shook his head and felt his nose starting to run and walked past his mother towards the stairs. He could still hear the scraping, the gritty sound of shovel on asphalt, but it grew distant as he ascended, and by the time he'd gotten to his room it had faded. He wondered if his mother had stayed there, next to the painting, herself lost in turn to the dress, the shirt, the brook; then the thought left his mind and he pulled off his boots.

Wednesday dinner, third Wednesday in the new year, Geoff asked the question. Or, more properly, Geoff made the request. "Tell me about the painting," he said.

"'Can you tell me about the painting?'" his father replied. "It's more polite."

Winter. An early dinner before his father would drive him to indoor soccer in the high school's gym, anticipating the sound of a thick plastic ball—air pressed taut against rubberized skin—colliding with the thin wooden walls, always threatening to crack them open. An early dinner so his stomach wouldn't turn when he played. Five forty-five brought chicken immersed in marinara sauce and a freshly tossed salad. The house was warm, an isolated beacon in a sea of beacons, a few holdouts of blue discernible in the sky.

"Okay," said Geoff. "Can you tell me about the painting?" He sat on adding "Please" to the end of it, as he knew how it would sound.

At angle to Geoff was Donna, not quite four. She grinned hugely and chanted, "The one with the boat?" She beamed; she couldn't help but beam. Donna shone and Geoff, by and large, glared.

"Not the one with the boat," their mother said.

114

"Geoff's fond of the painting in the hall."

"The one with the boat!"

"No," she shook her head. "The one with the boat's downstairs."

From the head of the table, a quiet cough. Geoff looked towards his father. "The painting," he said. "The painting goes back two generations in the family, to my grandfather." Fragments echoed in Geoff's mind: he could see parts of the story coming as through ancestral memory, as though this story of his great-grandfather was something he carried within him, a hidden organ biding its time within his chest.

"My father's father. Born Welsh; came to Toronto when he was twenty. Lived there for a year, working at a bank. He'd walk the streets nightly, my father told me. He'd walk the streets and see artists at work sometimes. Bohemians. Sacrificing everything for their art.

"He himself had no talent for painting. But he'd sit with these men and befriend them—they had things in common, a shared education, a fondness for certain writers. An appreciation of the same aesthetics. He came to call three or four of these men friends, and when it came time for him to leave the city—"

"Why'd he have to go?" said Donna.

"Work. He went south to Chicago and made his way further south from there, then west, and then north again. When he left Toronto, each of these men made him a gift of a painting, and he packed all four for the trip ahead, treasuring them.

"Five years later, he'd fallen into debt. My grandfather was a gambler in those days, and he woke up one morning to find that his life had gone to hell. 'I'd put my

115

life in a broken suitcase,' he used to tell me, 'and one day I looked back and saw the pieces of it trailing behind'. And so he sold the first of the paintings, pulled himself out of debt, and took the railroad across the country.

"My grandfather swore he saw that painting thirty years later, ascendant on the wall of a museum.

"He settled in the east, fell in love and married my grandmother. And they came on hard times after they'd been married for a few years, just before my aunt was born. Their first child. And, though it hurt him to do it, he sold the second of the paintings. And with that money—for the painting had caught the eye of a rich man with whom he'd become acquainted—they bought a house." He paused for breath and looked his children in the eye.

"You've been to that house, you know. My father and mother live there now. Your grandparents.

"They raised three children there, a daughter and two sons. My uncle Jack died in the war—you know that," and he faltered for a moment. "You know that, right? I've told you that?"

His children looked at him, Geoff aware of it and Donna largely uncomprehending—died? war?—and he continued.

"The two paintings that they still had outlived my grandparents. One came to my father, and one to my aunt.

"There was a break-in at her house. August of 1972. They took that and her television. Who knows how much it was worth? Periodically I'd look for it, in periodicals and art books at the libraries. I used to sketch it when we'd go there for holidays, when I was your age. That was another nautical one, Donna, like the one you like."

"What's nautical?"

"Boats," said Geoff. "Something to do with boats."

His father nodded. "In the attic somewhere or the basement, I have a sketch of it–the prow, the figurehead cutting through the fog. A ship of war come back to port."

Geoff's father waited for the payoff, and knew that Donna would supply it. A second or two passed, brief hesitant moments where his wife and eldest looked at him, both knowing that he was poised, an actor in the wings listening for that critical cue.

It came from Donna: "And where's the fourth?"

"It's in the hallway," he said, and let the inevitable smile flow out onto his face. "Just behind you."

And with that, the family returned to their dinner and spoke not at all of the day just past or of the day to come. After dinner, Donna slept and her father read; Geoff was driven to soccer and, chasing down a ball that had spun into one corner of the echo-laden gymnasium, slipped and twisted his ankle. Screamed out in pain and was dimly aware of his own voice coming back in response. It would be the last game of that particular winter: the next month of Wednesdays were spent in the living room, leg swaddled, devouring books on history for no particular reason.

In college, Geoff is led to painting. With naked eyes he watches paint dry upon the canvas slowly, a perceptible quickening that becomes alchemy in his eyes. Mornings in Katherine's loft, a signet ring worn by her grandfather now part of the attire she calls her own. She sometimes speaks the years and archives of the Hadfield family, a thousand miles from Geoff's own kin. Geoff is led to painting and comes, on some level, to embrace it.

"You always liked green," she said one day. He had laid the canvas on the table in front of him and had his eyes inches above it. Geoff was washing the canvas in green, layers of deep green; he had heard her say color field one day. The image that formed in his mind came from an archetypal psych-rock record: waving pre-fractal fields and an overabundance of purple. Staring down at the canvas, he saw strokes and impressions that might have suggested grain to someone, someone other than him, but nothing else. "Field," he offered. And again, "Field," with a nod.

It was the afternoon, three on a Friday. Geoff arrived there after his class, today's session having to do with Guelfs. Katherine had left the lights off, and the late March sunlight drifted in and suffused the room. She sat in the corner sketching; fifteen minutes for a cheekbone; then the cheekbone discarded, starting again, half hour this time. Pencil and charcoal on grand sheets of off-white. He'd bought the canvases on the table himself, sampled supplies from her stockpile until he'd felt properly informed. Half campus thought he was in the art program, and the other half had thought so until they asked. You're in what? they said, never failing. No shit, voices trailing off, evaluating just how interesting this made him.

She worked at recalling anatomy; he simply arranged colors. It's coloring, she'd said to him one day. It's coloring the way a child would. He paused for breath and said carefully, Are you sure you mean that? And she'd said no. And later, apologized: I hadn't realized how that must have sounded.

Layers of acrylic atop canvas: sometimes a shell. Cover the other side, too; why not?

Eighteen months together as the sun shone through the dirty windows and they worked. He stopped for a beer and she stopped for a beer five minutes later. "Green fingers," she said to him. She had this wicked grin on her face: she pulled off the wit that he never could, spoke with a halting malice that made him smile instead of wince.

Geoff said, "Yeah" with a quick glance down at the digits in question. Katherine walked slowly to the couch, beer in hand, and slumped down in it. "Hell," she said. "I'm done for the day. I'm done."

"All right," he said. He took another sip from his beer. "I'm going to do a little more of this. I was thinking of maybe seeing Hal's thing play at nine."

She'd been looking down into her bottle. "Okay. Yeah, okay." She raised her eyebrows at him invitingly. "I'd like to see that, too." He sat back down at the table, the dropcloth and canvas entirely occupying his field of vision. Squeezed out a rich blue onto his pallet and transferred some of it to his brush, and began the work of irrigating the canvas. He stared at it, the loft's silence accompanied by the sound of Katherine's papers rustling, and his hand continued to move. Threadbare strands grew fortified; the blue was rendered bold and came to rest against the green, something like equals. He looked at the shore where one color came to sit against the other; his eyes wandered over the border he'd made. Finally, Katherine tapped his shoulder. We were getting worried, a warm look on her face. Could he read it? No; Geoff was an illiterate in the matter of faces, but he drew her close, or she did the same.

Later that night, or the next morning, hesitant. Moon and reflected streetlights now making corners of the loft glow. "I was thinking of something." What, she asked, her arm stretched across his back and down to his waist. "When you met my parents–the painting near the front door. Remember?"

She shook her head. "The one downstairs, I remember. Why?"

He shook his head. "No reason. Remind me, though, the next time we're there. I want to show it to you."

"Okay", she said. "I will." And for a second, for three seconds, his mind filled with the image of her seeing it. I like it, she might say, studying its shapes, its colors, its mood. I do.

Katherine asked why he was smiling, and Geoff shook his head as best he could. "Never mind," he said.

"Never mind?"

"Never mind," a smile on his lips.

An office in a sub-basement, a cryptic after-hours elevator code, an oversaturated fluorescent glow: these were the hallmarks of Geoff's graduate program. He'd apparently won them over in the interview and through the letters: professors and associates of Katherine's who'd agreed to aid and abet him in something that would take him five hundred miles from her. Despite the wit and charm in the interview phase and the glowing letters, there was the small issue of his lack of relevant academic experience, leading to at least three outright rejections and one additional effort that, ultimately, proved futile.

He was here, two months in, the word madness still

coming to mind, Jotted a reminder in his handheld, a hand-me-down from Donna—call *K. 8:45*. Rubbed his chin and felt ten days' growth of beard, enough at least to convince his colleagues that he wasn't simply forgetting the essential elements of good grooming. He was playing chicken with the concept of a beard right now, which was fine with him. He'd ride his bike home that night; the rides helped him to shave off the fifteen pounds with which the previous year had gifted him.

The clock told him it was nearing six. Geoff wondered if the supply store off-campus was still open, and if so, how long it would be until it was closed. In other words, did he have enough time to get there and restock his supply of blue paint? He could come back here for his tiers of research afterward, then break to call K. 8:45, then bike home.

Light danced brazenly across the surface of the concrete blocks in front of him, and he concluded: 6:30, and I can pull it off. He made for his bike outside, unlocked it and slung the chain into his backpack. Pulling on his helmet he went, chasing the sky's last glimpses of blue into an absent horizon. Passed six poplars, the wind remaking the contours of his face.

Art supply shop: a minuscule low rectangle fed by a parking lot that, viewed from above, was its inverse in shape. Hanging over it were another row of businesses; an insurance agent, dance studio, and gallery all called the second level home. Inside, rows of rescued display cases. Half the store bursting with paints in tubes and bottles; tools for those paints; material on which they could be applied. Another third occupied by the peripheral supplies, and in the rest, the fractional spaces, nestled odd fragmentary materials. He looked at figures to reference in lieu of live models; looked at the texture of something synthetic, let his eyes dart over framing supplies, the idea forming in his mind to isolate a favorite work of his–

Christ, he thought as the word hit home, was he calling it work now? This wasn't work, it was something to do in the idle hours, a complement, not work–and the thought was washed back out, enveloped by his take on Katherine–

Geoff had ten minutes; this he knew from the sign outside. And he wandered over to smaller canvases, took three in his hand, and heard a voice. "Hey. Geoff. It's Geoff. Right?" Loose thin sweatshirt, hair akimbo–the name formed in his mind–Harry. Harry from Delaware; the other–he put it together now–eastern state expat in the program. They had mutual friends, to the extent that he had friends here. Harry had a generally open face, seemed sociable, seemed to know something about something, or at least gave that impression. "You dabble?" asked Harry.

Geoff gave him his best smile. Katherine aside, no one else from his world knew about this habit, this hobby, this distraction of his. "I dabble," he replied.

Harry nodded severely. "I know the look," and held up a block of some shapeless colorless material. "I do."

From behind the counter, the announcement of five minutes 'til closing came. Geoff indicated the cash register and Harry proceeded with the smooth choreography of longtime teammates. Harry flashed a twenty and a ten, while Geoff withdrew a scuffed debit card from his wallet. "Plastic, eh?" Harry said.

"Way the world's going," and Geoff took his canvases under his arm. They made for the glass door to the outside world.

"You got some time to kill?" Harry asked, and that was all it took for Geoff to conclude that his stack of work could wait a night. Meeting new people and all.

"Thinking beer? There's a couple of places within a few blocks."

"I'm thinking about—craving, really—a nice shot of whiskey, to be honest. But I think you can get beer at most of the places I'm thinking of, too."

"You drive?"

Harry shook his head. "I live five blocks from here. Makes the whiskey go down easier."

The place they found was a quiet sliver with a nearly bare front window. A splinter of a bar sat ten thin men; that bar was flanked by two booths in the front and four in the back. Neither Harry nor Geoff recognized any students there, but neither did they see any of the other barflies they'd come to recognize from their time in the town. The lights hung low and candles topped off tables; if you moved through the room, you moved through a porous amber that seemed lent to the air. On the stereo, the bartender conjured up a new homemade mix every hour or so: languorous beats, washed-out guitars, voices hollow and holy. Upon first settling in, Geoff and Harry traded stories of bars whose musical selections had mined a vein of cacophony. Traded stories of experiences at the airport ninety minutes north of them: that first flight in to have a look at the place in Harry's case; for Geoff, a trip there on vacation years before. Traded stories of conversations made blurry by an overextended set of speakers: Harry bluffing his way through a five-hour date, Geoff learning that he'd just agreed to pay fifty dollars for a small box of monocles. "To jukeboxes!" "Fuck jukeboxes," said Harry. "I'm getting old."

Then they traded impressions of the program; then they traded stories of parties they'd been to here and elsewhere, triangulating the ones at which they'd both been present. Six weeks back, loft thing. Reading a few blocks from here. Quiet subtle show, yeah; the one in the apartment with the brand-new floors and the chipped grey paint on the walls. The one at the collector of house music's one-story rental. The condo that smelled like whiskey. The place that reminded them both of a carnival. It was Geoff's turn to buy a round when the clock read 8:39. He stood and looked at Harry.

"You mind if this next round's a little late?" he asked. He tried his best to trace each word as it left his mouth, make sure it was clear, that he hadn't already taken on the telltale slurring he should have seen coming.

"What's up?" said Harry.

Geoff withdrew his phone from his pocket and pointed towards it. "Need to call my girlfriend. Told her I'd check in." His words came to an end and he remained standing, feeling like something should have followed that. Slowly, he detected a drunk beaming emanating from his face.

He could see Harry start to grin. "I'll be here when you get back," he said.

Geoff nodded, and the slow turn towards the door came. He walked outside and felt the air, suddenly cold against his forehead. Found a place to stand and dialed Katherine's number, carefully touching each key. Remembered as he pressed the penultimate 8 that it was stored in the phone, that he didn't need to dial from memory each time he wanted to reach her. Two rings and she had it, with an exhaled, "Hey". He nestled against the dark storefront next to the bar and took her greeting in and returned it. Within twenty seconds, she had picked up on his inebriation.

"You're drunk". It sounded good when she said it. Even now, years after she'd first said it to him, there was that tone of indignation, wholly false yet sharply delivered, and he loved it. She'd wear the Puritan role, almost; set herself up as the moral high ground, almost, and pull the change-up on him when she wanted to. Rarefied occasions, leaving him almost reeling. A recognition that there were sides to her that he hardly knew, that the potential existed of sides of her that he might never come to know.

"I suppose I am," he said. "I'm at a bar. Guy from the program and I are enjoying a beer or two." On most days, his enunciation wasn't this precise.

"You're making friends," she said. "I was getting worried."

He leaned his head forward, the pavement below it coming into focus, and shook out a laugh. "I'm a sociable gentleman," and the laughter flowed more once this'd been said. He couldn't quite say why. She joined in the laughter for a while; they shared that across the miles and beneath the common sky. And then she said, "You should call me tomorrow morning. We should figure this trip out, and I don't think you're in the best condition for travel planning right now. Go and drink with your friend; I'll get you up tomorrow."

He knew she couldn't see it, but he smiled at her anyway. "Awright. I love you."

He heard her say "I love you"; he smiled again and hung up the phone and paused a couple of seconds before walking back through the door of the bar. The urge caught him, the urge took him and told him that he should go to her then, that night, find a car and go. That that night in particular, he should be with her. No sense of danger there, no premonition of a coming menace; just that loneliness, that sense that something essential to him, something he needed, was far off. He inhaled and stepped back inside.

Two hours on. Crowds had passed through the bar while Geoff and Harry owned their booth, commanding round after round. Geoff wondered where this newfound ability to process the drink came from. Baffling. It was baffling. Barkeep'd already comped them twice, which was unheard of; they pondered an upgrade in the quality of beer, but nixed the idea: the cheap beer had gotten them this far and the cheap beer deserved to stay. The lights dimmed even further, the air rendered a flickering blue, and they started trading stories, and arrived on the critical one: how they'd come to be there.

Harry was a lifer. "I grew up loving art—I'd always had great art classes growing up, and I was always the one who got the most out of it, who did the best drawings, the best watercolors, all that stuff. And one day I woke up to the fact that I loved it but I, you know, wasn't actually that good. Figure drawing did me in, shoulders particularly. I fought the fight as long as I could, denied the inevitable, and finally threw in the towel. But given that it was the only thing I enjoyed, I figured there had to be some sort of way to get close to it.

"Couple of years into it, I thought I hated the history part of things, too. Started coming around, though, when I got my hooks into some part of it I could inhabit. I'm a pocket expert, they tell me—"

"Who tells you?" asked Geoff. He hadn't intended to cut Harry off, and as those three words left his mouth he became murkily aware that Harry could quite possibly take serious offense.

Harry paused, processed, ran with it. "Smart people tell me this. I try to associate with geniuses. Geniuses who'll, you know, flatter me. Flattery works best when it comes from the intelligentsia." He paused, frozen in mid-gesture, and raised an eyebrow to Geoff. Geoff nodded. "Thank you. Anyway. These laudables, these notables tell me that when it comes to certain locales in certain decades, I am what some would call well-versed. Techniques, influences—who had what teacher, who'd stolen what from whom. Very specialized—very, very specialized. Say, Vancouver in 1920. Philadelphia, 1890. East Lichtenstein, 1793." He drew the names and dates from mid-air, a magician conjuring handkerchiefs.

"Bullshit," said Geoff. "No such thing as East Lichtenstein."

"Hang on," said Harry. "I must excuse myself for a moment."

When Harry returned to sit down, he indicated Geoff. "Your turn. Cards on the table."

And Geoff said, "All right" and told him about the painting. Harry sipped his beer minimally throughout, and nodded. At the end, he prompted him for more details about the painting: the relative realism of it, the specific pigments of the colors. The sense of scale, the size of the canvas. The artist's signature.

"Toronto circa nineteen-hundred one of your periods?" asked Geoff.

Harry shook his head. "No. Not yet, at least. But maybe I know a guy..." He shook his head. "Nah," he said. "It's a blind spot for me." And the night continued, two more pints and that question of trying for the third comp, and then…no, no was the answer to that, and so each made his trip home.

The next morning, before Katherine's call could wake him, Geoff was rung awake by a call from Harry. "I've been thinking about your painting since last night," he said, "and something sounds weird about it."

Hung over, Geoff tried to say something like, "Define 'weird'." It emerged as a sopping string of vowels, his mouth dry and befouled by the beginnings of a hangover. He coughed.

"It's probably nothing. Jesus, you must have a hell of a headache. I'll call later," and with that Harry was off; Geoff staggered towards the shower. As the water cascaded across his head, he thought of blue and green and brown, and his headache subsided.

"It's good you got here when you did," he heard, and the snow continued its fall. The cross-country direct had taken him there, a seven PM arrival from which he'd caught a southbound train. Now he was in the car with his father, with Peter Mullen, on that familiar twenty minutes' road between the station and the place he still found himself calling home. "Much more of this and they'll start closing the airports. You're damn lucky. You were cutting it close." Geoff remembered sitting in the window seat as they taxied towards the terminal gate, of watching the first snow begin to fall.

"Where I live," said Geoff, "I don't have much choice." He and his father had run this conversation through a series of permutations in the past. Geoff expected that this wouldn't be the last time they spoke along these lines; some part of him suspected that his father might be thinking the same thing. "Was different when I was an undergrad–more roads home from there."

Peter smiled but did not face him. "Maybe. Long roads, though."

"You know what I mean."

Peter let out an elongated "Yeah" and slowed the car. "Christ," he said. "Your mother will be livid. It'll take us at least an extra ten minutes to get home, probably fifteen. Slow going in weather like this." Geoff rested the top of his head against the passenger-side window and watched the interplay of snowflakes and light: their headlamps, streetlights, the handful of lit porches they passed. Virtually alone on the road, they were doing twenty-five where forty would have been adequate several hours before. Geoff biked nearly everywhere out west; he wondered if he'd need to drive in the three days he was back. Six days until he'd next see Katherine; one until he'd see Donna and this fellow of hers, about whom he'd heard much.

Seven minutes to the house now, accounting for weather. Geoff let out a cough. "Dad," he said.

"Yeah?"

"The painting in the hall. You mind if I take a picture of it before I go back west?"

"Why?"

"Guy in my department was curious about something. A friend of mine."

Peter drummed his right thumb against the top of the wheel. "Curious about what?"

"The style of it, I think. I told him the story of how we'd come to have it, and he..." Geoff stopped. He'd spent the flight east and the train ride south phrasing this out in his head, but the words nevertheless seemed flawed. Was there a right way, a proper way, to ask this question? He measured his father's terseness, the silences and the coursing of the wind above the car. "You've probably thought about this, too. You might have, at least. He said that someone on the avant-garde around those years, wouldn't have been doing that sort of work, that my description of it sounded too representational. It sounded too representational to him, at least. It could have been my description of it," and he felt himself losing control of his words, his line of reasoning losing traction and coming to rest somewhere unexpected. "I honestly don't know. We talked about it, figured a photograph would be the best measure of things." And then another, "I don't know." He hushed quickly, regretting this phantom retraction.

Peter grimaced and again knocked his thumb against the top of the steering wheel. He did this again a minute and a half later. The cabin of the car felt brittle, and Geoff wanted nothing more than to turn on the radio, to draw sound into this space. As they approached the development in which Geoff had grown up, Peter looked at him. "Practice," he said. "All it was." Geoff looked at him, his mouth half-open to demand more information, but his lips went silent, and Peter offered nothing else.

In silence, the car crossed the driveway, the snow already enveloping the asphalt below. "I'll shovel this after dinner," Geoff said.

"All right," said Peter. "You don't have to, you know."

"I know," said Geoff. "But I miss doing it. As strange as that sounds."

Peter shook his head. "Fair enough," he said. "I'll lend you my old jacket. Should fit you, right?"

There were days Peter could have passed for a much older brother of his son. Their frames were alike in all but their carriage. "Definitely," Geoff said, and they stepped out of the car, each reaching into the back for a suitcase.

The snow had tapered off by the time dinner was through, leaving a few inches to coat the yard. Geoff and his parents sat and talked for a while, the remnants of their meal congealing atop their plates. They spoke of neighbors, of the extended family, of work and school and the coasts. And then Geoff excused himself and, taking his father's worn jacket with him, walked to the garage. He caught sight of the painting out of the corner of his eye and smiled, knowing he'd return to it later in the evening.

He opened the garage door that led out to the driveway and chose work gloves and a shovel from the wall, the same one his father had used when Geoff was a boy and that he'd come to use after reaching a certain age, when snow days stopped being entirely for leisure. He stepped out into the cold, precise night and fell into the old movements after a few loads. He felt the skin beneath the work gloves shift, and knew he'd have blisters in the morning. He didn't mind: this repetition beneath a rose-blushed sky calmed him.

He cleared the path first for his mother's car, which he'd walked past in the garage, then carefully stepped back up to finish the work left by their tracks from earlier in the evening. His father's car, a rich brown color, sharply contrasted the blue of the house. He inhaled and exhaled and stood for a moment, mesmerized by the sight of his breath hovering above their front lawn. He came to the back of his father's car and dug under the snow next to it and threw it onto the lawn, then stepped slightly and repeated the motion. It wasn't his father's technique; Peter had in fact chided his son for the impracticality of it, but Geoff had timed himself once and compared it with his father's under what he believed were similar conditions. To Geoff's mind, the results of each were identical.

Half an hour later, he had come to the end of the shoveling. Most of the driveway's surface lay exposed, and he walked back to his father's car to rest and let the night sink in. He knew no one else back in the old hometown that night, and thought about how he'd spend the next few hours, before sleep could even be considered as an option. Curiosity took hold of him and he reached for the handle to the trunk. It was unlocked, and he raised it above his head slowly, gently, so as not to shake any excess snow loose. Inside he could make out the edges of a number of wooden frames. He lifted them and, in the dim light provided by the trunk's solitary bulb, shifted them so that their images became clear.

Eight paintings total, two copies each of a set of four: the painting from his childhood, the nautical scene he'd seen his father sketch and two others that he did not know. A ship's prow, crossing through mist, familiar in its outlines from sketchpads; a man and a woman standing in the distance, framed in a doorway, two sets of brush-strokes in his hands identical to the ones he could summon up at a moment's notice. Gently, he set the paintings down and touched the surface of one with his fingertips, felt the dried paint, felt the need to twist it, to wrench it somehow. He pulled his hand back. Geoff heard the front door open and halting footsteps on the path leading to the car, the paintings, him. Words fell to earth unspoken. He stood there, a light dust of snow newly falling, and sang to himself: exhale.

SPENCER HANGS OVER NEWARK

1.

Somewhere near seven hundred feet, Spencer looks down at the seaport of Elizabeth, streetlights like pinpricks in a child's planetarium. The 737's wing angles down by minute degrees, reaching out towards Manhattan as the plane makes its final approach. The airport beckons, a harbor of new glows and old concrete. He opts for the window seat just behind the right wing whenever he can get it for this moment: looking back over his shoulder at the ground, gazing at industry in miniature. The slumber of oil refineries, cargo loaders, outlet shops. The diminished motion on the Turnpike now that the day's commutes have ended.

He hopes the rental will be waiting for him with a minimum of wait time. Couple of years before, he'd signed up with a few of the agencies, reluctantly put his vitals on file. That abbreviated wait helped to coax the lull into something manageable, something that reduces the old anxieties and apprehensions into a dull white noise, a simple shrieking, easily ignored. Six hours airborne—nine by local time—and another ninety minutes on the road; at least another ninety. The lone downside to this seat, he thinks, is that, barring an empty flight, you're always one of the last to leave, standing hunched over, stray strands of hair flirting with the fans and reading lights.

Spencer dwells in the moment and doesn't regret his choice. He's always traveled light on these trips. A gym bag in the overhead compartment, a novel or two and a shaving kit. If he's lucky, if he's played time right, he'll pass a K-Mart or Target or shopping mall on tonight's drive to his destination. He'll get the casual clothes there, the $8.99 three-pack of boxers, the navy blue socks and thin white undershirts. Maybe stand there a while to savor the nine p.m. crowd and share in their exhausted feeling of displacement.

He'll buy the suit in the morning, as he's done in the past, and again thanks his maker that he rarely needs tailoring. Shipping costs to send it back to Boise are always high, but the line item on the monthly bill is innocuous enough. He understands this: his method is far from the easiest way to travel. Spencer doesn't care. It's his preference to do things this way, and he can certainly bear the cost.

Below, he sees trucks and cars the size of gnats, tiny globes of light at the end of poles. Sees buildings, perfect squares and circles fringed with rust, mats of green dividing them. All rendered in a clear night's shadow, colors muted, their motion precise and determined. He can't shake loose the feeling that their speed is somehow wrong, that the highway's 65 miles per hour have had their danger stolen from where he's sitting. Consider vantage the thief of velocity.

He reaches into his pockets: wallet in his left side

pocket, keys and phone in his right. Spencer is aware that he can pack his keys away until his return: the house keys and car keys and office keys from Boise will open no locks in the Garden State. And yet they're there, present because of the wet panic he feels between the moment when he reaches down and detects their absence and the onset of remembrance: *keys on the table, keys on the dresser, keys in the duffel.*

It's January. Bitter cold outside, he knows, and a bitter kind of cold back west as well. He'd told Alice almost nothing, alluded to a business meeting; his company had offices out here adjacent to military bases of a certain size, so the explanation was certainly plausible. In the pit of his gut, he feels the plane turn and descend at a faster rate, his stomach seized by a rarefied sensation of motion. He breathes slowly, skull tapping out something like a prayer, to slow this moment.

Whenever he stands to use a plane's bathroom and begins his walk to the rear of the cabin, he feels intuitively that he is walking on something less substantial than the floor below, can sense the tens of thousands of feet beneath his feet and the surface of the earth. It never fails to quicken his heartbeat, as though a step to the wrong place would reveal the inherent illusion to the floor, would send him on a quick descent through the clouds. That sensation never quite leaves him until now: that final movement of the final approach.

Ten years ago: he'd been back east for a conference, had found himself wandering near the old hometown. Late-night coffee at a Starbucks, reading a copy of the Register he'd bought earlier in the day. One of three patrons at that hour, the light brown wallpaper reflecting the hanging lamps' mid-range luminescence. Patterns tattooed on the walls evoking a nautical womb, a maritime sweat-lodge stripped of the discomfort. Going section by section through the paper, skipping the national news and delving into local politics, sports, and the like. Reaching the birth announcements after an hour, skimming it to see if any names looked familiar, if any middle-school pals or lost loves had become parents in the past few days.

And it was then that he saw one of the names, one of the Names: Alphonse Tilden. A wildcat dread hit his stomach at that moment, and he knew—knew before the research, before the phone booth and the ersatz stake-out—that Tilden was one of them. Spencer added a day to his trip within the hour, put miles on the rental car he'd never relate to a soul. Sat in the rental outside a hospital for three hours, drinking soda and reading a biography of Harry Truman. Finally, the doors opened and Tilden stepped out. Spencer saw his face, saw his head from the proper angles as he turned to go, and received the necessary confirmation, his memory coldly embracing the moment.

Spencer had taken down Tilden's address from the phone book. Upon his arrival back home, he dusted the wallet off, made sure that it was free of all traces of him, replaced the twenty-three dollars that had lain within it that day in '73, and mailed it anonymously.

It had been a broiling hot God-damn July at the fair-grounds near Newark. Spencer up there with Alec and Ray, all of them fat pampered kids, barely seventeen, thinking a little danger'd be a good thing. They thought it'd be smart, be keen, to make a minor-league ruckus. It was something they barely knew how to do: they'd been bullied once or twice, thrown into lockers; the near-miss boys' room fights; the staredowns after the last bell rang, walking towards the buses parked outside. Spencer and Alec and Ray had all been kids who looked away first.

Stupid kids, naïve, without any idea of how to make a proper ruckus.

The fair near Newark: Alec and Ray hinted at things, feinted like they'd start something; Spencer called them on it and they eyed him and said, Well, what've you got?

And Spencer walked cold out through the fairgrounds, sweat wringing his eyes into squints, and stole a guy's wallet. Walked past him, saw the back pocket bulging, and reached, pulled. He figured the guy'd be onto him in a second, all of a sudden start wailing on him, but no such luck: he'd gotten it clean. Briskly, he walked deeper into the crowd, pulling three more along the way, Alec and Ray a hundred feet behind him, two hundred, gaping.

They dubbed him Spencer the Klepto when he got back, and it stuck long enough. Kept the money for themselves, tried to get beer but couldn't quite pull off the look to buy it. Ended up making a half-assed run to A.C. and getting laid up in Seaside instead, spending a weekend on the boardwalk, acting fake-tough and praying they'd find someone who'd sell them some beer or gin, something in a bottle to get 'em all wasted. Down there they were anonymous, no story before that moment, no preconceived notions except their own. They'd tried acting like the kids who'd stared them down, adopting gruff demeanors and glaring at one another and saying, "Awright kid, you're going down tonight". They could pull it off for maybe a minute and a half before one of them would bust up laughing and call Spencer a klepto and he'd say Yeah? And who got us the money for this? There'd be a pause and then, Fuckin' klepto! And the laughs came, and it was all right.

Alec joined the Navy a few months after college and vanished. Ray stayed local, drank hard and ended up on probation by '77. Spencer had sent him a card last Christmas, but the gesture had not been reciprocated. He hadn't anticipated that it would.

Below him, the miniatures grow larger. The airplane's rate of descent always amazes him, a traversing of thousands of feet, seemingly at minuscule increments, and yet the final hundreds pass in a moment. Cars and buildings now rendered at a one-to-one scale, earth's plane made tangible. A forced communion with one's fellow travelers, the impending hive-mind rush to exit the plane a singular concern. Traveling light meant you didn't have to reach into the compartments overhead, could simply reach under the seat in front of you and procure all that you needed and make for the plane's doorway, passing the smiling pilot and the congregation of flight attendants watching you leave.

That moment, by Spencer's estimate, is ten or fifteen minutes away. He gazes back over his shoulder, feeling a barely discernible sensation of falling, and again sees the vaporous lights of industrial New Jersey. It's a train-set, he thinks, a model train-set, and wonders for a moment if that's something his sons would like, if he should bring something back this time. He puts his family out of his mind then, detaching himself from his life in Boise, his home, job, car. He's a portable man for the next few days, a device with one purpose.

After the return of Tilden's wallet, Spencer devoted the occasional Saturday to seeking out the remaining three Names. He kept the wallets in a locked box in his desk and, after an initial cleaning of all three in conjunction with Tilden's, never looked at them.

Recent years had been better for his efforts. A wedding announcement in St. Paul gave him a lead on Mikal Devore, and a passing mention of Nicholas Bester in an Austin, Texas news story had not gone unnoticed. In both cases, he fabricated a convincing reason for travel, observed each of these men, knew his instincts to be accurate, and made the anonymous mailing from back home.

Richard Leblanc had been harder to locate.

Web searches, phone books, and the usual avenues turned up nothing. The thought entered Spencer's head that Leblanc could be deceased, but a revitalized search of obituaries and death notices was equally fruitless. Spencer tried as best he could to keep the process from interfering with his life: searching only at home when his family was elsewhere, taking the occasional lunch at the library a few blocks from work, and developing an anonymous email account for any and all correspondence related to the project.

In the autumn of 2003 he found his answer. It came, unexpectedly and unwittingly, from an aspect of his home life. Although they had met at a conference years before in Kansas City, Alice's hometown and his own shared a state; a two-hour drive was all that divided them. Her cousin Raymond, an attorney more than a decade her senior, had been staying with them over a long weekend when a call had come for him. A news story, Raymond had explained later, about a case he'd handled as a young public defender. A con man and counterfeiter who'd broken the nose and jaw of his arresting officer; they'd locked him up for years, fights within the prison walls affixing more time to his sentence like trailers to an office building.

"I had some bad ones," Raymond had said, "but this guy seemed all right. Wicked temper, though. Wicked Goddamn temper." And then the rueful shake of the head. Raymond was a virtuoso at that. "Guess that's what did him in."

This prisoner—the pugilist and forger—was due to be released in a few weeks. He'd be arriving back to society as a man in late middle age, reformed but for all practical purposes lacking a place in the world to which he could return. A reporter from the paper would be profiling him, hence the call for Spencer and Alice's guest. Alice, who was fond of such information, asked the prisoner's name, and it was then that Spencer learned where Richard Leblanc had been for those many years.

Spencer hangs over Newark, closer to the ground now, hoping that the landing will be smooth. He smiles as he thinks of the cold outside, imagining it scrape across his face and hands as he walks to pick up his rental. He never packs gloves when he travels in the winter, not for these trips or any others.

Tomorrow he'll wait for Leblanc to step off the bus, he'll confirm things and make the last return. He had planned initially to confess, to explain everything when he reached the last of them, but a new idea has come to him. Thirty years ago, he withdrew wallets as smoothly as one might swim through a sea of milk; thirty years later, can he unmake that gesture? Can he replace things as easily, as pristinely as he once extracted them? Tomorrow, he thinks, it'll be over. Spencer's never been one for credit. He and Alice are both well-paid for the work that they do, and financed their home themselves. This, for him, is the last marker he's carried forward through the years. The thought of being free from it is a momentary echo of a peace to come. The plane approaches the gate, and Spencer is ready to stand. He wonders if, perhaps, he shouldn't just look Leblanc in the eye and explain himself as he hands back the wallet. Perhaps they can shake hands and find somewhere to eat, a small diner with cheap food a stone's throw from the water. There they can sit and talk and compare their crimes. All his debts paid in full, he tells himself. All his debts paid in full.

2.

Spencer reaches the rental car office twenty minutes after landing, sees the line before seeing the logo, sees that there's a wait simply to get inside. It's eight forty-five on a Tuesday, the middle of January, and this line has gathered on the wrong day: it's a holiday line, a Thanksgiving weekend line. Quarter-hours pass and he draws closer, seeing a harried clerk carrying out separate transactions on three computers, fingers and legs spelling out polyrhythms. Spencer hears mutters of disgust from the line behind and ahead of him, hears bags dropped and shifted from hand to hand. A man four ahead of him sings along with something on his headphones: not a song Spencer knows. Twenty after nine, and fifteen still precede him.

Eventually, he makes it to the head of the line, receiving an apology and a set of keys from the man behind the computer. This time through, he can't walk outside to retrieve his car: it's parked inside, forty steps from the counter. And so only when driver and car have left the garage can Spencer lower the windows and allow the cold air entry. It shears his face as he goes, raises the hair on his arms, and it's the first part of the trip since landing that has met his expectations. That it's now past ten o'clock means a change in plans; itineraries will need to be realigned: wake earlier, acquire the basics, back to the hotel, shower, change, eat. Then, he tells himself, a drive south and a suit.

His finger hesitates over the radio as his car moves down the Turnpike, speedometer wavering around 70. The stations are never the same, he thinks; the ones he likes always change formats while he's away from a particular place. He longs to find something familiar, a song or voice from his last trip to this part of the world, but a survey of the dial offers nothing. His plans for the night still reshaping in his mind, Spencer considers a detour to the old fairgrounds, slows and maneuvers to the rightmost lane, but then regains his former position. It was Alec who had driven them all up there; Spencer hadn't watched the road in those days with the zeal he currently possesses, and he realizes now, wind still buffeting his forehead, that he would have no idea where to go.

Fifteen miles later, Spencer pulls into a rest area, coffee and a sandwich on his mind. Flying nearly always leaves him famished, whether or not a meal is included with the airfare. He steps out of the car into the freezing air, closes and locks the door behind him, and stares upwards; it's only in winter that the sky in this part of the state gets so clear. He hears vehicles in transit going both ways on the Turnpike, sees the occasional headlight beams of cars following his lead, and observes travelers, solitary and in pairs, making the trek back outside. He rubs the side of his face for warmth, a solitary standing figure in the midst of subtle motion, and turns towards the entrance, its glow saturating the night.

Halfway through his grilled chicken, Spencer notes that he and the other patrons of the fast food alcove here are all facing the counter. Their positions have no discernable logic, but nonetheless: all face the counter, and each sits alone. His own vantage is from one of the tables furthest back, and as his glance travels the room, he takes in a series of backs, quarter-turned faces, each wholly absorbed in their own action. He recalls Leblanc's face now, last seen as a similar sliver: loose chunks of straight hair, a white t-shirt, and eyes that were not brown. Above him, a fluorescent light shivers. He looks back up towards the counter, sees the last server on duty begin to close up. Spencer holds tight to the image of Leblanc's face in his mind: over Spencer's own shoulder, a fraction of another man's face viewed from over his shoulder. He clings to that half-remembered face.

Back in the car, he turns on the overhead light and looks at a map, eyes focusing on a particular cluster of towns, tracing his route, remembering names and locations of hotels. He and Alice had contemplated a trip out here for his twenty-fifth reunion. At the last minute, they had backed out: Alice was concerned about leaving the boys unattended for so long, and he felt a surge of relief that he needn't run the risk of bringing her among people who'd known him in his wilder years. He turns the light off, starts the car, and shifts into reverse, savoring his memory of maps.

Forty minutes later, he's taking a familiar exit off the Parkway, making two fast turns, and then he's there, he's reached the hotel, he can check in and call it a night. Six minutes to a K-Mart that opens at eight, provided the traffic's good. Breakfast sandwich from somewhere, to be eaten on the road–factor an hour twenty of southbound driving to be in Absecon. And then what? Wait for the bus; watch for the reporter and the man with the camera. Spencer checks in to the hotel bag in hand and asks the woman behind the desk, in passing, if there's somewhere nearby where he can get a drink. On the way up to his room, he decides against it: the novel he was reading on the plane will quiet his nerves well enough. Inside the room, he charts the following day's trip: seventy miles of the Parkway, morning light on his face the whole way down.

The trip to Absecon is perfect, lifted from his schedule and rendered across time and distance. Ten o'clock finds him at the state's coastal fringes, where the land frays and drifts towards the Atlantic. He turns the car inland: five miles to the closest shopping mall. Any evidence of a rush hour has passed by now; he passes a few school buses on the Black Horse Pike, but nothing more. Leblanc's wallet sits in the passenger seat beside him.

Spencer minds the time as he enters the department store. As he settles on the right and proper fit, his eyes return again and again to the watch on his left wrist, each potential suit thinning the time before Leblanc. Three options are winnowed down to one, and Spencer ventures back into menswear for a matching shirt and tie. Once he's paid, he asks if he can return to the dressing rooms to change. The man behind the counter gives him the okay but can't help but ask about the occasion. "Something personal," Spencer says.

As he's adjusting his tie, it occurs to Spencer that he has given the impression of a man headed for a funeral, a memorial service, an early wake. The suit's dark enough, and Spencer knows his demeanor at this moment: anticipation, apprehension; a sense of duty, of obligation, and above all else, closure. He recalls the tone of his words spoken minutes before, and those words and the manner in which they were said are clarified to him. Consider misdirection as mocking the true funerals, memorials, and wakes he's attended in recent years. He feels blood run to his cheeks and sweat on his brow. Once finished he makes for the counter, meaning to give a fuller explanation. But the salesman he had spoken with is gone, nowhere in sight down the racks of shirts and shoes, and when Spencer steps outside and feels the air attack the sweat beaded on his forehead, he savors it.

By eleven-twenty he's waiting for the bus to arrive. He realizes that he had been wrong about the presence of a photographer: there's only the reporter, young and clean-shaven, adorned with notepad, recorder, and digital camera. The reporter is leaning up against the side of the bus shelter, staring intently down the road. Spencer, parked twenty feet away, considers joining the watch. Grey inches into the sky above them, accenting the harsh winter light as it nears its apex. Spencer forces his eyes closed and then opens them as he reaches for the door handle, setting his feet onto the pavement as stronger daylight floods in. He inhales as he turns towards the bus shelter, slams the door closed, and checks his pockets for both his own wallet and Leblanc's. He walks towards the reporter, keeping his distance. The reporter looks up at him and says, "Waiting for Richard Leblanc?" And Spencer nods his head, waiting for the reply. But the reporter doesn't: he only nods his head in silence.

Spencer has checked bus schedules, has pinned down times in his mind like horses in a photo finish, and now he feels his heart in his ears as he waits. He glances again at his watch: eleven twenty-two. One more minute, he tells himself. Braces for the reporter to confirm the time, to make small talk, to interact with him in some way; but no, the reporter is silent, fingering the settings on his camera, adjusting the white balance, contemplating a scrawl on his notepad and adding a few more. Eleven twenty-two on a weekday: no early-shift lunch traffic to be seen. Spencer eyes the road and sees motion on the horizon, but as the speck grows larger it resolves into a compact car, navy blue, a solitary man inside. More motion a minute and a half later: this time, a white pickup and a grey sedan moving in tandem.

The bus pulls up two minutes after that, and Richard Leblanc is the only passenger to disembark.

Spencer takes the whole of Leblanc in: his back still straight, a few inches shorter than Spencer, thin build, wiry then and wiry now. Thick glasses over red-stained cheeks. He wears a winter coat, unzipped down the middle, and paint-stained khakis. Of all of Spencer's Names, time has been the least kind to Richard Leblanc, but as Spencer stands there watching, he realizes that that was to be expected. His heart's resonance is now a tattoo through his bones. Leblanc is a handful of feet away and everything else–the reporter, the bus, Spencer's own form–loses substance. There's only Leblanc's modest form and the pounding, an echo turned inside-out. Spencer hears, "How do you feel?" and it brings everything back. Words rush into in his mind, form pages upon pages, before he turns slightly and realizes that the question is Leblanc's to answer. Disappointment hits his throat. Leblanc says nothing, and the reporter volleys back with a question on work. Does he have a job now? Somewhere to stay?

"A hotel," says Leblanc. "Cousin of mine has work." He eyes the reporter for a second and continues. "I'd rather you not say which. Could make his life harder." And then Leblanc's eyes drift over to Spencer. "You got a light?", spoken in a lower octave. Spencer sees Leblanc's face clearly now, pale green eyes and a few dark strands left in his hair. He freezes, recognizes Leblanc as the sort of man who threw him into lockers in high school, who could stare him down, no questions asked.

"Sorry," Spencer says, first to look away. "Sorry; I don't." He wonders what the reporter makes of this, but won't turn back to see.

Leblanc gives the ghost of a shrug. "That's all right."

He returns to the reporter, asks if he has anything more.

The reporter says, "Nothing for now," takes one more photo of Leblanc, then walks to his car. Spencer again confirms Leblanc's wallet in his pocket and looks into the distance, away from Leblanc and the photographer. Hears, "You're not with him?" Leblanc's voice sounds diminished, fading with age, but even so it can summon up a force to beat back memory.

"No." Spencer turns back towards Leblanc. Spencer's rental is the only car in view; fringes of grass covered by leftover snow bracket the sidewalk, and both are held to account under the barren sky, neither with any apparent reason to continue speaking. Spencer says, "You need a lift?" and it feels hollow as it reaches his ears. How can it sound to Leblanc, he asks himself. It can't sound right, and yet suddenly he hears Leblanc agree, hears himself asking if Leblanc is hungry, hears Leblanc acquiesce, and as they start towards the car it comes to him that Leblanc's probably been in stranger positions over the years. Immediately, Spencer loathes himself for the thought.

They're sitting in a small Jersey diner now, ten tables at most, half-full with the lunch crowd. Sitting opposite one another in a booth large enough for four, neither having spoken since they entered the car. Leblanc's jacket hangs on a hook above his left shoulder. As Spencer picks apart pieces of a chicken salad, his eyes move to Leblanc's arms. On both, ascending towards his sleeves, he sees a series of scars, as though a crude ledger of time was carved into his skin. Leblanc, devouring a hamburger, doesn't seem to notice Spencer's stare.

150

When about a third of the burger is still uneaten, Leblanc abruptly speaks, both elbows on the table, hands supporting his forehead. "They let me out when I stopped fighting." His eyes don't leave the table. "And I stopped fighting when it hurt too much." He breathes deeply and resumes his meal. Spencer looks down at Leblanc's hands, knuckles scarred and busted, pale thin lines across his fingers, scars he'll bear until his death.

Spencer does not reply, and Leblanc offers nothing more. Spencer sets his fork down and wipes the corner of his mouth with a napkin; that he sets down as well. Leblanc methodically finishes his hamburger and moves to the rest of his food. As Spencer watches him, his eyes drift to the handful of people seated behind them, and he wonders if they recognize Leblanc. He observes the wait staff moving quietly among the tables, his gaze coming to rest on a tired older man stepping out of the kitchen and sitting at the lunch counter for a few minutes, head down, breathing deeply. Spencer suddenly feels aware of his suit, of how at odds it is with everything around him: a formal statement in a space with no use for formality. He loosens his tie and unbuttons the top button of his shirt and sets his hands on the table, waiting, looking at every square inch of surface around him. Fifteen minutes later, a handful of fries still on his plate, the coleslaw half-gone, the neon still burning above, Leblanc says, "You can get the check if you want."

Spencer signals their waitress and leaves twenty-five dollars on the table. Both men stand and walk towards the door, Spencer in the lead. They pass a glass-and-metal cabinet full of cakes and pies on the way out, the side facing them mirrored, and Spencer catches sight of his own face in it just as Leblanc enters the reflection. Two men, an abundance of lines on their face, hair gone to grey, a weariness somewhere; he thinks, we could be family, and curses himself for the comparison. They step out the door and into the afternoon.

Spencer says, "Do you need a lift somewhere?" and Leblanc shakes his head.

"My cousin can get me here. He's not far off."

And Spencer says, "All right." Breathe, he tells himself, breathe like a normal person. He reaches into his pocket and pulls out Leblanc's old wallet. "I should be giving you this," he says, and hands it over. Leblanc takes it cautiously, his eyes moving from Spencer's to the burden in his hands. He opens it, slowly surveys what's inside. Spencer watches his face, training himself in that moment to detect any signs of recognition, but sees none. Leblanc thumbs through the wallet, noting the currency, checking the feel of the leather. No emotions cross his face: neither nostalgia nor elation nor hate.

Finally, Leblanc looks up at Spencer and begins to open his mouth, just for a moment. No words come, and he closes it again. Spencer can see something form in Leblanc's eyes but can't interpret it; it's an expression that never dwelled in his lexicon. They stand in the sun, Leblanc with a pay phone in arm's reach and Spencer closer to his car, each waiting for words. It's Leblanc who breaks the silence first: without malice, he looks Spencer in the eyes and says, "Go home". Not a warning, not meant as a command; a benediction, Spencer thinks. A benediction. Spencer nods and swallows and then says, "Good luck," as he walks to his car. He looks back at Leblanc twice, each one little more than a blink in time.

As he pulls back out of the parking lot, he sees Leblanc put the wallet into his side pocket, sees him pull change from the same pocket and initiate a call, and by then Spencer's facing the highway adjoining the diner, anticipating his next turn, the traffic grown more dense.

Spencer reaches the second hotel of this trip an hour and a half later. He changes out of his suit and stands at the window watching the descending sun blur colors at the horizon. He sees a pool covered up for the season, no chairs for families to relax in, no students standing guard over it for summer salaries. Spencer picks up the telephone, pauses for a moment, and dials Alice to tell her where he's been.

STANTON STAND, SEES, STARES

1.

The first thing young Stanton saw when he crept into the den was the light of the television; the second, that his father had fallen asleep on the couch beside it. The third was what was happening on the screen: a woman, dirty-blonde hair tied into a loose ponytail, adding dough to a human-shaped form on a long ceramic countertop. She further honed it, giving it traces of a personality, giving it quirks and irregularities and bending it at odd angles. Then she left the room, and slowly the shape on the counter changed; over the next twenty seconds, the image dissolved between neutral dough and flesh, until a man sat up on the counter and slowly took his feet.

To Stanton, this passed as though he was watching a dream. He felt a short stab of terror run through him, an unmoored quality; that same feeling he got on the beach, watching his mother pass beyond the waves, even if only for a moment. That terror that she might not return, that he would be left stranded amidst strangers in depths of his own.

The man made from bread, Stanton saw, didn't seem to know that he was made from bread, and so he began to wander through the streets of a small town. He met people; he sat and drank coffee at an outdoor cafe; he exchanged jokes and gazed wistfully at a young woman in the distance. And when the day was up, he glanced at his hand and then watched as it turned back to bread. Life ebbed from him and he became inert, carted off by the woman who'd first made him.

Stanton sat and stared and wondered just what he was watching. Eventually his mother found him and carried him to bed, and it would be sixteen years before he saw the show again.

2.

The rental car's GPS spits out fractured directions, turning street names into dismantled sound-art. As he drives, part of Stanton wants to record this, to play it back and pass it off to a friend back east to transform into something lucid, something dubby, something dense in which to lose oneself. Right now he's content to pass the hotel for the third time and focus on how the GPS voice intones "La Cienega Boulevard," words accented in an alien manner, the syntax of no nation. Passing the hotel for the third time and the hedge-lined entrance to UCLA for the fourth, daylight waning, streetlights starting their illumination and the night's roadwork taking shape.

This will further fuck the directions the machine gives him, he understands. He'll be told to turn right on exits shuttered until the morning; he'll need to improvise, will hear the inevitable chidings of the synthetic voice and will proceed through them. He wishes he understood the roads of Los Angeles better, but there are no patterns here; no easy conversions to a grid as there are in New York or Portland. He's done for the day with the academic conference, finished with the paper he'd come here to present. And now he's circling, making loose loops around the campus and the hotel in which he's decamped and trying to lock on to a destination, a restaurant at which to eat or a venue that holds a promising band. In the absence of those, he proceeds in fits and starts, traffic his chief obstacle.

In the end, he ends up at a record store.

At a party before he'd left on this trip, he'd found himself in late-evening conversation with a woman named Lena. She'd turned the topic of discussion around to metal, had volleyed names and references at him, of which he'd recognized only a few. He'd found her beguiling, and he'd wanted to pick up on a few of the things she'd suggested in the hopes of earning her admiration, of moving towards a common language. Because it was preferable, he realized, than talking about his area of expertise, the area in which he was on track to earn a doctorate: an evaluation of certain television programs with an eye towards the limits of the body and transformations of the same. All born from an opaque series of dissolved frames: nascent dough overlaid with the flesh of a lifetime.

3.

He parks down the block from Amoeba Records and puts an hour's worth of change in the meter and approaches the front door. His hand seeks his right pocket and finds a few more quarters; he reverses and returns to the meter and feeds it the rest of the change. The sky will be well into darkness by the time he exits, he realizes. He's fine with this.

The store has a span like a warehouse or a small hangar. A row of cashiers and a security guard and the bag-check window all line the wall to his left; on the right, the space expands into something cavernous. Parallel rows stocked with music extend out of Stanton's field of vision, and above them are signs ticking off the names of genres, demarcating formats, separating new from used. He ventures off in search of metal; he thinks he's in the new release section, and it's only fifteen minutes later, after he notices a general absence of certain contemporaries, that he realizes he's been browsing used music the whole time.

Before that moment hits him, he goes looking for Wolves in the Throne Room and instead finds a cache, three columns deep, of Warrant. It seems to Stanton that two of them are comprised entirely of *Cherry Pie*—were he seeking their earlier album *Dirty Rotten Filthy Stinking Rich*, he'd need to shift positions, trek further down the aisle. There are rows of them, all proclaiming that cover: red-haired model dressed as rollerskating waitress, her legs beginning to awkwardly splay, the cherry pie of the album's title falling, caught by shutter or after-the-fact manipulation to be positioned just below her waist.

Stanton remembers his year and a half of Warrant devotion; of listening to the title track again and again. Of playing it in the tape deck of his father's car—that and the Damn Yankees album—on trips to the Brendan Byrne Arena, trips on the Palisades Parkway, trips to aquariums in Brooklyn and Camden. In retrospect, he's tempted to call his father—tempted to call him from this very spot, no matter how awkward it may seem—and apologize. Then the impracticality of that strikes him and he knows that he'd be in the stranger position of apologizing for incidents already forgotten a decade earlier.

Mostly, when he thinks about listening to "Cherry Pie" and talking about *Cherry Pie*, he remembers conversations with his friends during that brief time when the bulk of their interest in music was all concentrated on one slice of metal, abundant with brash boasts and long solos, and where the inevitable power ballads offered the promise of slow dances in middle-school gymnasiums.

And then there was his discussion of *Cherry Pie* with a friend, when his friend had brought up the cover. His friend had grinned and looked at it and said, "You know what it means, right?"

And Stanton had nodded and said sure.

And his friend had called his bluff. "Okay. What does it mean?"

Stanton can't remember exactly what he said in response, and for that he's grateful. He does remember that look on his friend's face, half hilarity and half contempt, and can very clearly remember the mocking he took in the days and weeks to come. Certain words and phrases still remain lodged in his head, specifics that his subconscious periodically dredges into the light.

In the end, he stands in the used metal section's "W" area for far too long, his stomach rumbling, his eyes unable to look away from the legion of covers. He does sort himself out; he does make his way to the proper section, and he does engage in a not insignificant amount of commerce before he goes. In the end, he finds that the extra change had been most necessary: only ten minutes remain on the meter. He punches his hotel's address back into the GPS and waits for more shattered words to come forth.

4.

Two days later, he gets a call from some college friends about a concert at a small art space a forty-minute drive away. He has groups of friends from three distinct eras out here: a small cluster from his hometown, names and faces who would recognize the Stanton of the Warrant tapes and Damn Yankees tapes and mild distrust of Great White; a larger group of college friends who might nod their heads appreciatively if he brought up his reason for being here, who might find some common thread between his pursuit of half-remembered childhood television and their own cultural sweepings; and a trio from the job he'd held briefly after graduation, before he had pressed himself back towards advanced degrees and long hours spent decoding culture. These were friends he had known from a loft space where gleaming furniture was degraded over the span of nine months: wear revealing design flaws and shoddiness of materials, and reducing the workspace from catalog-photo ready to a case study of entropy.

It is the collegiate group who have called him, promising a singer-songwriter whose manipulations of sampled melodies offer the opportunity to witness the gestation of nostalgia into something unexpected–their words, halfway cribbed from a press release, not Stanton's. The conference that day had been illuminating, but had left him feeling spent by evening's arrival. His colleagues had divided into distinct groups, and Stanton had felt himself on the fringes of all of them; he had paused and waited for them all to make plans and had failed to pursue any of the open avenues. And so he sits in the hotel room watching the last vestiges of daylight drain from the sky and curses his own indifference.

As he waits there after receiving the invitation, he considers. He calls one friend back and agrees; Stanton can hear the uptick in his friend's voice, can hear that anticipation of anticipation, and wonders if his own matches it. After hanging up the phone, he gathers together his things and walks towards the parking lot.

When the first interstate meets the second, the skies open with rainfall so loud it drowns out the GPS's own haggard voice. Stanton slows the car from sixty-five to forty, the assault on the windshield grown percussive and frenzied. Of course he's brought no umbrella with him—he has not, in fact, brought one on this trip at all. He scans looming buildings in the distance; flat warehouse-sized spaces full, he assumes, of shops where some cover can be bought. But by the time he's exited the highway and found himself in the home stretch of his voyage, he sees nothing open, just shops shuttered for the night and darkened strip malls and a handful of restaurant-signage neon. He zeroes in on the show's site soon enough and decides to circle for five or ten minutes in the hope of an all-night mart in the surrounding blocks. Twenty minutes into his circling he's found nothing, and has almost skidded into the side of a minivan hastily exiting a strip mall, deserted for all but the nighttime security.

Stanton slides the rental car into a parking spot four blocks from the concert space and considers. He will, he knows, be soaked by the time it would take him to sprint to the venue's entrance. There is no shelter looming above this pavement, no areas of refuge from the unflagging rain. He envisions failing encounters with friends last glimpsed three or four years ago, all of them immaculate even as he resembles someone saved from drowning.

He checks the forecast on his phone to see if he can anticipate a break, to learn whether a decision to wait the weather out might be in the offering. No, he learns; this rain will last all night, only abating in the small hours to come. He sits in the rental car's seat and lets the decision settle in; he pulls up the name of one of his friends on his phone and keys in a repentant message. SORRY, he types. THOUGHT I COULD MAKE IT BUT THIS WEATHER'S KEEPING ME CLOSE TO HOME. Only half a lie, he thinks, and sends it off.

5.

The next morning, a text appears on his phone: WATCH THE NEWS. His heart flattens and he turns on the hotel room's television. There's been an earthquake not far from where he grew up, he learns. Stanton watches images of damage in old haunts and hears reports of cracked buildings and shattered roadways near his current home. He sees things stunning and unforeseen. The northwestern part of his home state squats in ruins, buildings leveled, variations on a desolate theme. Newly formed jagged skylines recorded on shaky phone cameras are magnified and stretched to fill the television screen.

Calls to friends and relatives reveal silence on the lines, the phone company squelching out strange noises to signal signal failures. Phone calls to dead air lead to phone calls to automated messages lead back to phone calls to dead air. Stanton goes to the last day of the conference and sits through it numbly, those colleagues of his gathered around him now rendered alien, his fellows but no longer his peers. He extends his stay at the hotel for another day, then for another two.

He makes it back east in fits and starts. Stanton lives for four days at the airport in one Midwestern city, where he is persuaded to board a train that he's told will get him within a hundred miles of his destination. He accepts the offer and boards the train and finds its progress halting and ultimately too frustrating to continue in this manner. These become the weeks of trickle charges in his phone, of an earned familiarity with new smells summoned by his body. He learns to shed and to streamline, handing books over to other travelers as he finishes reading them, leaving pungent and unsalvageable undershirts in public restrooms and sliding credit cards to purchase more.

Stanton returns to the east coast three weeks after leaving the west. Not long after that, he abandons his apartment. Steps towards his thesis are left on hold, an indefinite leave of absence is granted. He calls family, makes an offer to help with the rebuilding, finds it accepted. And so he proceeds back to his old hometown, driving a decade-old compact car through once-intimate streets. A town far enough from the epicenter that it wasn't ruined is still jarred in certain subtle ways: trees upended and three crucial buildings now laid to waste. A shortened legacy and the promise of bile now serving as a point of unity for the residents.

One afternoon he drives to a new chasm. He has heard talk of rivers newly emergent, of centuries-old buildings and hovels recently uncovered. There has been talk of some new land birthed from the horrid contortions of the old. He drives as close to it as he's permitted, and walks a hundred more feet. He stares out but sees nothing revelatory; Stanton sees the earth after an up-ending, but little more than that.

He finds the television quietly, watches programs that arise after the late-night programs have ended. Stanton watches series airing at three a.m. without context. He stares at the pictures and seeks out images on which to linger; sometimes he turns off the sound and turns on the captioning and waits for the two to fall out of sync. He waits for that unfamiliar feeling to return, that transition and transformation around him. He waits for its presence, its opposite of reassurance, and sees nothing but lost shapes drifting into the night.

His parents sleep in a room rooms away, its door closed; as he walked past that door hours before he could hear the sound of bodies snoring. Who is there to wake, he wonders from the couch. More honestly: who is here now for him to fear waking? The revelations here are familiar to all of those he's rejoined. He draws memories and theories and interpretations close to him, looks to walls and windows, sees nothing that could be called clear. Sees rigidity without logic; sees patterns without pattern. Stanton's night passes, his eyes awaiting a signal, awaiting a greater sky, walls to fall away, some new mystery to appear.

THE INDEPENDENCE SHIPPING COMPANY

1.

Another long day's trawling. I am thankful for the ship. Thankful for the chamber and thankful for the coastal views. Maine at its northernmost. Lost miracles before we set out for the resting spot, the contented spot. Captain tells us we'll make Miquelon this run, that we've taken on the proper space, the proper weight; that our stint in the shipyards was not for naught. I ready the power source and plug in and begin the night's words.

Songs of the colder months. Songs of jackets and parkas, all of us remaining for the fall and the winter bound up in them on deck, awaiting our brilliant piercing views of towns shuttered for the season.

We have been told that there will be cabins in Miquelon; that visa arrangements have been made for the overwinter stay there. I'd signed forms in Grant's office before I boarded: a room a little larger than mine, a divider set up between living areas and the space where he did the ship's business, archaic communication technology scattered on countertops and wall-hanging in harnesses. Something that looked like my mother's cellular phone, an immaculate relic now decades old. "That?" I asked with a nod.

"In the waters we travel, service is strange" he said. "Sometimes you stay with the classics."

I didn't envy his works. When we would disembark for the handful of supply runs in Bar Harbor or Saint John—the captain and I taking most of the pickup work, my cost of travel—it was Grant's time to barter for contracts, for annotations, for notarizations across all borders. He was often the last to board. I would watch his furtive runs down the docks, the gait of a man sprinting to avoid a downpour, even when there was no rain.

***

Eight of us had bid for this life, and three were selected: two for the crew, and me to document it all. The captain insisted on a print volume. Grant preferred the notion of electronic dispatches, either archived somewhere or sent sporadically, a newsletter that advertisements and appeals for cash could be affixed. Grant knew better than the rest of us what the ship's condition was. There had been benefits before we cast off; there were ambitious plans for this vessel to be the first of five, the first of a fleet. So far, it was the first of one. We had been given our territory to monitor. I observed and jotted down impressions, images, interviews. Ate eggs on toast. Imagined tricks to make the bulk-bought coffee taste better.

The northernmost bookstore in Maine is two days' voyage off. Some books will be offloaded; I read during the six days I'm off shift; a constant barrage of words. I sit in the waiting area, near the space that had served as cafeteria when this ship was an operational ferry. There are few of us now, few enough that seats near the counter are the source of no competition. We can dwell there fine.

Most days I sit and read and study. I journal. I look at old maps and dream of the coastlines. We're the new voyagers, I suppose. We're keeping watch.

Two days until new books, and until I can hand off some of the old. Over the radio comes a broadcast telling of a canal between the New Brunswick/Nova Scotia border; a way to circumvent coming too close to Halifax. I heard the captain clear her throat. "Lies," she said.

"I know," I told her. "You don't have to tell me about the landscape." She shook her head and went. The charge on my light lasted for a little longer. I dimmed it further and walked outside and looked out at the railing. I saw silent cliffs and breakwaters, and gulls' slumber on the rocks. I saw buildings in the moonlight and in the searchlights, but I saw no forms in the windows. Early sleepers, I thought, or abandoned. I returned to my cabin, and to the maps there, and dreamt of old exploration.

2.

The older man is back. He rejoined us in town; we docked, bartering some items and bringing new food on board. The captain had said some words about gardening, of using some unused space on the deck for a kind of greenhouse, a shield from the cold and the spattering salt from our transit. Since then, we have heard no news. Perhaps it will be begun in the warmer months; regardless, this docking, six hours in total, resulted in no building supplies being brought back on board. I went there quickly; I dropped off some books and bought a new stack of volumes for this, the leg into international waters, and the long wait.

I was reading in my usual seat when the older man rapped on the wall above me. It should have been startling; instead it was enmeshed, as much of the structure of the space as the creaks of the deck and the sound of splashing from the waterline. "Still here," he said.

"Still here," I said.

We called him "the older man" because of his seniority to Hector, The Old Man, who'd been one of the first to join the vessel. Hector had been 75, a fit 75, a spry 75. He had made one of the long circuits with us during the time that we still made the long circuits, before Halifax turned hostile. We picked up the older man, who'd once asked us to call him Vilgrain, at a dock that had long since vanished from our routes. He'd spent eighteen months on the vessel and then he'd gone. "Time of two births," he'd said to me once, and I'd shrugged. Plenty of encounters with the inappropriate, but fewer out here. We imagined ourselves stoics; we imagined ourselves better, a self-selected society. Who knew if it was true?

One day, I expected to be an Old Man, or an older man. These passages seemed to be what I did best. A passenger; an observer; and, sometimes, a set of arms, a set of hands. A counterweight.

The older man passed along an unsolicited recounting of his time over the past few years. There was an abandoned school, he said, where his daughter lived with her family. He'd lived there for a few years; he felt the call of the ocean, he told me, and said his goodbyes. He seemed to have packed light, and I suspected that his stay this time would be a brief one, before land called him again. Still, there was always a place for alumni here.

The older man knew that as well as anyone.

The night after he boarded again, we met; he had brought a bottle of mezcal with him from the mainland. "The family hates this stuff," he said. I was amenable. You didn't see many spirits out here; you didn't see many drinkers at all. The roll of the deck, the salt in the air, and the monotony all drained us. You dehydrated easily; many swore off more than a handful of drinks per week after their first shipside hangover. There were the "blue flames" as well: the travelers whose reaction to the chaos was to drink themselves insensate each night, until they ran out of whatever bottles they'd amassed and decided the seafaring life was no longer worthwhile. They'd disembark at whatever port we stopped at next, duffel bags by their sides, hoping for a room at a hostel or guesthouse. The blue flames rarely returned.

The older man sat with two tin cups before him. Ice within had summoned condensation to their outsides. He pushed one towards me. "How's it been?" he said.

"Sparse," I said. "You're the first to return in months."

"Hm," he said, and took a sip of his drink. He hadn't swallowed it, I saw. He had opted to savor. For my part, I drank mine right down and let the burn resonate in my throat. "What've you seen?" he asked.

"Nothing but shoreline and cabins," I said. "Nothing off in the deeper reaches. Just the chop and the birds that fly behind."

"Amory still fishing?"

"Amory left two months ago. Bought a bus ticket on his laptop and said he was heading to Portland. Either Portland."

The older man took another drink and rubbed his

forehead. "That'd be it for the fisherfolk, then?" The older man talked like he was navigating a fantasy world half the damn time. I'd never seen him reading, but Amory had told me stories of his room: secondhand mass-markets most everywhere. Which wasn't a statement of economics: most of the bookshops we saw in the towns where we docked trafficked in used volumes. We rarely went as far south as Portland; we rarely stopped near Acadia, and I was one of the few on the ship who could remember a time when we'd docked in Halifax.

We traded stories, the older man and I. He had worked engineering systems for six months on the mainland. Said there was a grand-nephew who'd talked of taking buses up through Canada towards Alaska, crossing the border and crossing the border. He'd heard there were boats similar to ours there, the constant motion, the ocean underfoot. The grand-nephew had been inspired, tantalized.

"You didn't warn him off the life?" I said. "You know what this is."

The older man shrugged. "I spilled my life to him," he said. "Told him of the grit and of the hungers, but also the glimpses. Kid was drawn in by the glimpses."

All I did was exhale; hoped that would signify my disapproval.

"Rumors the kid had heard, too," said the older man. "Rumors it's better in Alaska. Sightings more than glimpses."

Maybe he was right. I'd been on the ship for too long to want to take my chances on Pacific waters, to say nothing of the traversal out there, broke-down trains or long buses, halfway to nausea for hours on end, the jostling making it near-impossible to read. I was fine out here, chasing those glimpses, my words before me.

3.

Felt blocked for the last 36 hours. I never stay on a good cycle out here, and I've been out here long enough that it's harder and harder to remember if I was ever on one that was proper. Prosperity tormented me; that and the rock and weave of the boat, the sound of the crashing. My last time landside I'd fallen asleep to the sense of rocking. Two days of shoreline life hadn't broken me of the sensation that I was still out on the water; two days after getting back onto the boat, I still felt land's unsteadiness beneath my feet. It was a hybrid state that I'd come to despise, a loathsome epidemic.

If I ever exit this craft, I'll need to contend with it again. But for now, I'm on the water for the foreseeable. I have my dwelling; I am amphibious.

I shudder when thinking of life back on land, further depleted of the belongings I already culled to make this voyage. I imagine myself inland and decrepit, all traversals ended. That hybrid dizziness my default state. Those godforsaken goodbyes all I have to my name, and after a while, not even those.

Dreamt I was flirting with the captain. If I had friends there, we could laugh about that, and the inherent dangers of such behavior.

The captain and I had joked about it once: photographing the Lights to fund our activities. We crowdfunded adequately; the allure of these coastal trips was often enough to pull on board an affluent patron every six months or so. We trotted out ceremonies for them;

we ferried them on board via a powerboat through the shallows, upped the drama, sold the vessel's size, made it look imposing rather than the converted commuter ferry it actually was. The captain often suggested we do the deep runs then. Much of the damage we took was to impress the donors; that too was a part of the routine. That sense of breaking it and buying it, by which I mean, yes, the captain was damn good at guilting the hell out of the wealthy and getting a little extra for fuel, for the stockpiles, for the gear we used to measure conditions and hope for a return of the Lights and the messages they carried.

So, then: the Lights and the shapes that emerged from them. This was the phenomenon we stared at, and the downtime we kept along the way. We got dispatches from the shore periodically, like cloistered monks getting news in quarterly increments. I'm sure some could fixate on the Lights and see evidence of aliens and others the divine and others new and inexplicable developments in climate, of the way light hits the atmosphere. Dim shapes in the Lights that might have been letters in some lost language. A cryptographer's paradise. We had some come on board once. It was a disaster, as some had predicted. Shouts and questions of the captain's authority. Attempts to take the vessel below the Lights. There was, in fact, no way to do this.

4.

Some fuck boarded with a satchel of books on the monastic tradition. Talked about pitching a tent on the lower level, where this vessel had carried cars when it had been a vessel that carried cars. For my money, it was dangerous. Now the arrays from the panels on the roof were down there, along with the plants and the tanks. When I walked through the upstairs platform, I flattered myself by thinking I could differentiate the rumbles each of them left in the walls.

Who was the fuck, I asked the captain. Consultant, she said.

I asked her what kind he was. She smiled. Line of succession, she said. Keep this thing going if the krakens take me.

Krakens aren't real, I said.

I know, she said. But who the hell knows if I want to captain forever.

She was keeping this sustainable, which I well understood. Still. Borrowed a bottle from the older man, told him I'd repay him when we next docked. That would be, someone said, the geodomes at Winter Harbor. Pretty sure one of those was a general store now. Stragglers last year told us someone had begun making variations on gin. Almost no-one's gone blind, they said. So I would do that, buy one for the older man and one for me. For the present time, I kept to myself; I let the ship's rocking steady me, and I thought about the next.

5.

Crossed into Canadian waters yesterday. Saw another vessel, with Moncton registry. A couple of us stood on the platform and waved. The whole crew seemed to be children. Didn't seem right. I assumed someone older was at the helm, but all the wavers looked ten or eleven. Children of the crew, I supposed, or some sort of strange daycare. Or maybe they'd hijacked the whole thing; perhaps we were one fragment, bystanders in their adventure. I never knew with kids. You didn't banter much with other vessels. It was months since we'd seen the last converted transport vessel. There were plenty, but the schedules never lined up.

Maybe there weren't plenty any more. Who knew? I didn't man the radio here. The captain would know such things, and some of the crew. I had other duties. When I did take on labor, it was usually private. Made me something of an outlier among the crew, but I didn't mind.

I saw the captain a few hours after the Moncton ship had passed. What was all that, I asked. She shrugged.

Maybe a generational thing, she said. Maybe an apprenticeship.

Seemed rational. I asked her about the next destination. We hadn't docked in days. She said, somewhere between here and New Glasgow. And then New Glasgow. I nodded. She asked if I had a preference. I said didn't. And then I amended: anywhere I could walk on land for a little bit. Not just the pier systems; somewhere we could have an hour or two to wander. I hadn't wandered in a while.

She said, I'll see what I can do. Which probably meant we'd stop at Port George for half an hour. I was all right with that.

6.

Port George was shrouded in mist, as it always was. The old buildings that overlooked the water; the summer cottages, no longer inhabited seasonally. There, too, were the modular homes, a more recent addition, and the artists' studios, some small and some cavernous. Art was one of the industries here now; it was also a port, albeit a modest one, pulling in vessels like ours and selling spirits, dried meats, packaged goods. Reports of bad weather to the north meant that we'd dock here for the night. I was all right with that. Sleeping with a different sort of motion below me seemed fine: that steady rock instead of the unpredictable forward momentum.

I dropped off a few letters to you. Seemed preferable here than from the States. Unsure why. Maybe because we were in the Commonwealth now, I suppose. I walked to a general store and handed over the letters to you, and a few postcards to distant friends. I thought that I might purchase some more. I asked the proprietor if she had any. None left, she told me. Maybe if we stopped here on the return leg. Seemed fair, I said.

I walked up the hill to get a few of the vessel, to get a view of the town, to get a view of the open water. I'd bought some ground ginger from a shop beside the general store, and steeped a pinch of it in mug of hot water. It felt calming. The sun had started to set, and I saw something stretching along the horizon. I wondered if we might not be due for an installment of the Lights tonight. I wondered what the captain would tell us once we'd all boarded the ship again to bunk up for the night. Or most of us: one of the others often bunked with someone when we passed through here. I envied her for that.

Dirt and rocks set below my feet. I was a thousand feet from the limits of the town. There were a few small shacks here; a couple of tiny homes that had been ferried out here on crafts sturdier than ours. It had been a while since I'd last looked at the structure that I'd called home for so long. It seemed good to see it in a landscape, to see it with surroundings. When I looked back at Port George, it seemed less like a vessel docked there than another building, closer to the waterside than most. That seemed welcome. That seemed a kind of pleasure. I watched it move ever so slightly, the current's tremble conjuring a resemblance to seismic action. The thing seemed rigid, but also not.

I took out my old camera and took a photo, and then another. I'd have something to send to you in the next letter, or I wouldn't: salt and time had ruined more rolls than I'd like to have imagined. But still, that image. The passengers we conveyed looked up for their preferred signs; mine came off the shore. Mine came from low-lying buildings and the craft near them, and the sea beyond. I stared at it for a little while longer before starting the walk back to the ship.

7.

We docked in Port George for another two nights, and then struck out again. A viewing of the Lights, and then on to the winter. The guests would disembark in St. Pierre, as was the case ever since the local government in Halifax turned hostile. And then Miquelon, where the remnants of the crew would dock for the winter, lodging in one of the dormitories for the coldest months. It was a profitable arrangement for all involved; it was also one of the few times you'd see multiple vessels in a single space. It was a strange and temporary society.   You   saw some of the same faces year after year; others came and went. Some, you knew, didn't have the taste for it. Others had opted to start families, or to venture into other lines of work. There were plenty of reasons to cease life crossing these cold waters.

Still. We all stayed in an old factory: the rooms were heated but a central courtyard stayed seasonally chilly. We would gather there and drink spirits in the cold, or head to one of the town's taverns. We didn't feel archaic so much as timeless.

There were romances there; some brief and some that lasted. It was a good and heartfelt place to meet, I'd always said. The old factory. The walks through cold streets and the echoes of French spoken by the residents. If you were on the seas for a year or more, you picked some up. You had to.

Mail went out infrequently. Connections for phones or laptops were intermittent. It was a place of relative isolation, and I was okay with that.

Two months there, maybe more this year. I'd see the new faces. I'd see who'd come, who'd been on the ships after all the dignitaries and clergy and philosophers went away. It was a welcome season.

8.

Four days out of Port George, we saw the Lights. I was drinking coffee and eating something dried when I heard the bell's somber ringing. Usually it was the captain who did the ringing; sometimes she'd delegate it. Once, I'd been standing beside her when they came in sight on the horizon: the patterns in the sky, the absences in the middle. If you were to ask me when I first felt connected to the ship, it would probably have been there. The hand on the cord, then hearing that sonorous sound traveling throughout the ship, and hearing the movement of feet towards the deck. That sense of causation, and the mysteries off in the distance.

I had a mug of coffee in my hand as I walked to the deck. Out of windows, I could see the Lights in the distance, already huge, occupying much of the sky. I walked to the deck; I saw the Captain there alone, the rest of the crew, the rest of the visitors, standing on the opposite platform.

Will you miss this, I asked her. You know you'll miss it.

She smiled, was all.

The absence in the middle of the Lights doesn't have an explanation. Some of the clergy and prophets say it's a message from something divine. Codebreakers analyze the shapes in them, the forms. They think they're letters, and maybe they are. Maybe they're nonsense. Maybe they're someone's art. But when I look to the sky and see the Lights, I see a correspondence, I see something up there that maybe isn't meant to be read. But still. We perceive it. We watch it and we hope we can make sense of it. And I sit down and write, letters to a you I don't even recognize. I watch and I wait and I hope, a year from now, ten years from now, to still feel that strange sense of connection.

SOME THINGS I BOTCHED

1.

There was a prompt in front of me and the prompt said "write the saddest poem ever." I read words three and four as "saddest porn." Cue fourteen explicit pages with a subplot of dying puppies. It cost me some friends. Maybe more than some.

2.

Before that, there might have been some good news.

3.

There was the Dixieland jazz band that became a grindcore band. Elderly avant-jazz heads told me I was the fastest clarinetist they'd seen. I basked in this, believe you me.

4.

Also noted: the faun I nursed back to health. He lay beside the highway one night when I drove by. Feeding him wasn't so hard; house-training was harder. Harder still was hiding him from the hunters: that sound of hounds barking outside, the sequential knocks skipping from door to door, the horns in the hallway.

5.

I latched on.

6.

There had been a relationship before that. There had been a we. Then, for a month, all my pillow talk involved mascots. Then there was no we.

7.

Contingent with the clarinet, I gave juggling a try. The band began touring. Bassist Alexi was driving when one sphere grazed his eye. My juggling gear was jettisoned on I-80. There were stern warnings given.

8.

We would hit the road for long weekends: Chicago, Boston, Richmond. Once we linked up with a subway grindcore band called We Stop At Five Dollars. The open road and rest stops. Moonlight clarinet and exhortations to violence. Speedy exits.

9.

The sound of a banjo gone supersonic? You could build a religion around it. Last I heard, bassist Alexi was trying exactly that.

10.

Airfare was booked. The Czech Republic beckoned. The festival circuit loomed. We had an audience there, we were told. An eager one at that.

11.

Three days before we were set to fly, I got a call. I'd been replaced. Someone better. Someone fitter. Someone who could also play the oboe. Someone who didn't juggle; someone who, at least, didn't juggle hazardously.

12.

Six days before we were set to fly, I saw the writing prompt. I went to it. Something saddest, I read. I thought: I can manage that. I thought: there are brilliant fragments still to make.

13.

I follow my former band's itinerary. I feed the faun his oats; we watch the stars. The hunters haven't shown in weeks. Cue the sound of cicadas; cue all the damage you can muster.

LINER NOTES + CREDITS

Winter Montage, Hoboken Station

In the winter of 2010, I was house-sitting for friends who lived in Jersey City, in an apartment located close to that city's border with Hoboken. Because of that, I ended up taking the PATH train to and from my job in Manhattan from the transit station in Hoboken where the story is set. I found myself getting somewhat obsessed with the fact that there was a very small bar in one corner of the station; the idea of two people meeting in this out-of-the way place appealed to me. It didn't hurt that I had a couple of odd connections with the building: a former employer of mine had been involved with the efforts to renovate the ferry terminal located there, and my maternal grandfather worked for the Erie-Lackawanna Railroad, whose name adorns one side of the building.

To exit the terminal and head to Jersey City from the PATH station involves passing several rows of parked trains. One day, when passing them, I looked up and saw snowflakes slowly falling through a hole in the roof. That image stuck with me. Later that night, I sat down at my friends' apartment and started writing; eventually, this story emerged.

The Wenceslas Men

The books that made me a reader involved a good dose of the uncanny. I read plenty of science fiction and fantasy and horror when I was a teenager, and my initial gateway into more quote-unquote literary works were generally through books that incorporated some aspect of the weird, speculative, or surreal. (Examples include Thomas Pynchon's *Gravity's Rainbow*, John Crowley's *Little, Big*, and Margaret Atwood's *The Handmaid's Tale*.) But as a writer, a large amount of the short fiction that I wrote for a long period remained firmly realistic.

In 2013, I was asked to take part in a cosmic horror-themed reading that Alex Houstoun was putting together at WORD in Greenpoint, Brooklyn. This gave me pause, as I wasn't necessarily sure that cosmic horror was something that I had it in me to write. But I remembered a second-story apartment that I'd visited briefly the previous year, and the way that I had looked out a window and briefly imagined seeing someone walking there as though they were passing along on the sidewalk. From there, a story began to emerge.

What struck me the most about this, though, was the impact it had on my own storytelling. It reminded me that there were a vast array of tools that I had at my disposal that I hadn't been using. It didn't mean that suddenly, every story that I wrote was going to feature something paranormal or bizarre in it—but it did mean that I had many more options for storytelling going forward, and that the best way to tell a certain story wasn't always to stick to realism.

Last Screening of A Hoax Cantata

In 2013, to coincide with the release of his novel *The Absolution of Roberto Acestes Laing,* Nicholas Rombes invited a group of writers to contribute pieces to Necessary Fiction. One of the options offered was to write about a fictional film, and that was what I ended up running with. I thought back to some of the genuinely bizarre things that one could stumble across in the days when VHS was the primary medium for video. I remember seeing a video that seemed to be some kind of bizarre blend of performance art, industrial music, and experimental cinema. I've never been able to find any reference to it online in the years since then, and I keep wondering if the whole thing just vanished from reality around 2005. The story also provided me with the opportunity to write a bit about the part of New Jersey where I grew up, albeit in a slightly fictionalized way, and that was fun as well.

Airport Hotel Ghost Tour

In 2011, I traveled to New Orleans. It was a quick trip: I flew down on a Friday afternoon, and took a very early flight back to New York on the following Monday morning. For the first two nights that I was in town, I stayed at a hotel near the French Quarter, which put me in close proximity to a host of great restaurants and bars. I was unsure of how long it would take to get to the airport from there, however, and so I booked a room at an airport hotel for the third night.

This was not one of the wisest decisions of my adult life. It isn't to say that there was anything wrong with the hotel–but after a couple of days of being introduced to a great city, spending one's final night there eating chicken fingers in the chain restaurant downstairs from your room is something of a step down. "Well," I thought, "at least maybe someday I can work this place into a story."

A Record Called "American Woodworking"

The record referred to in the title is a seven inch by the band Policy of 3, released in 1995 on Old Glory Records. (The songs later turned up on a discography released by Ebullition in 2005.) Policy of 3 were a fantastic band and are well worth your time, if music with an abundance of guitars and pained vocals is your thing. The story's inspiration itself is sadder: it emerged out of a trip to Seattle, where I saw an old friend who I hadn't spent time with in a couple of years. Over the course of our conversation, I learned that a mutual friend had died a few years earlier. I'd had no idea, and learning about that cast a strange mood over the rest of the trip: the elation of travel spiked with time-delayed grief.

Yannick's Swiss Army

I became an ordained minister in the Universal Life Church a few years ago, thus giving me the ability to officiate weddings. (As of this moment, I have officiated none.) Slowly, I wondered what would happen if someone used that ability for nefarious purposes: a wedding-officiant super-villain, essentially. That idea ended up blending with my habit, for a few years, of showing up at my local soccer bar to watch Tottenham Hotspur games roughly twenty minutes into the first half. There are also a few nods in here to the Modern Lovers song "Pablo Picasso," which I was first introduced to via John Cale's version by the same friend responsible for introducing me to Tottenham several years ago.

You In Reverse

Sometimes idle ideas stick with me. For instance, after missing a subway for the nth time: What if I just reversed my personal flow of time and took a train going the opposite way? I borrowed a title from Built to Spill for this one. This is not the first time that I pilfered Doug Martsch's discography for a title, and it's likely to not be the last.

An Old Songwriter's Trick

For an as-yet-unwritten project, I had a need to get one of that project's two main characters out of New York and on his way across the country. (For more on that, see the notes for "Dulcimers Played, Strings Played.") That character was Owen, and this story began as a reason for why he left New York. It turned into something else, though. I first came to New York to study film in the fall of 1995, and in writing this story, I was able to revisit the East Village of the late 90s and early 00s, which was both enjoyable and bittersweet.

It also let me do some things that I had always wanted to try out in fiction: a narrator who wasn't the story's protagonist, for instance. And it allowed me to use a couple of ideas for stories that had been floating around in my head for the contents of Owen's films. Owen is, very much, a character to whom I can assign a number of bad ideas that have run through my head. Every once in a while, though, he also gets a good one.

Party Able Model

THE2NDHAND was one of the first journals to accept my work, for which I remain eternally grateful. After "Spencer Hangs Over Newark" was published, I was asked to take part in two "mixtape" readings, one in Chicago and one in Brooklyn. This was the story that I wrote for the Chicago one, inspired by the Joan of Arc song "A Party Able Model Of," from their 1998 album How Memory Works. I did not know, at the time, that Joan of Arc's Tim Kinsella would go on to become a major part of Chicago's literary scene, which is a fine thing indeed.

Dulcimers Played, Strings Played

Eccentric minimalist composer Henrik Phebes shows up in one other story of mine, "Every Night is Bluegrass Night," which didn't seem like an ideal fit for this book, but may well end up in a theoretical second short story collection. (I say "theoretical," yes, but I should confess that I already have a working title for it: *Selected Ambient Fiction Volume II.*) The character of Alyce plays a much larger role in a novel I keep meaning to write, in which a disgraced filmmaker travels to the Twin Cities to shoot an adaptation of G.K. Chesterton's *The Man Who Was Thursday* on the fly, with the 2008 Republican National Convention as the backdrop. That disgraced filmmaker would, in fact, be "An Old Songwriter's Trick" protagonist Owen–who, you may notice, is last seen venturing off from New York City to parts unknown. I initially wrote that story to get a better sense of Owen, and it slowly became its own thing. Funny how these things work.

I didn't have a title when I finished this, but I'd been listening to a lot of Labradford's 1999 album *E Luxo So* as I was writing and editing it. I glanced down one day to see what song was playing, and noted that it was the album's third track, "Dulcimers Played By Peter Neff, Strings Played." (The album's six songs are named, somewhat arbitrarily, for the credits.) And with a bit of editing, i had a title.

Why I Was Not In New Jersey For Christmas In 1997

During the year of its existence, I read at the Difficult to Name Reading Series twice. Once, the theme was holiday-related, and I wrote this story for it. It's a blend of two distinct images. The account of working on a film and venturing down to a friend's apartment near South Street Seaport while I was increasingly delirious from a 24-houg bug is all true. (I was, in fact, so out of it that I boarded a Brooklyn-bound train going home and then wondered what the hell I was doing at the High Street station.) Years and years later, I dreamt that I got on a subway and heard, via an announcement, that it would be running express to Los Angeles. I have very few dreams that are both coherent and exciting enough for their imagery to be worked into stories, but this seemed like a perfect fit.

Western Bridges

This is the second story written for one of THE2ND-HAND's Mixtape events. The song from which it takes its inspiration is "Winter on Ice" by The Spinanes, a song found on their 1996 album *Strand*. I should probably take the opportunity here to argue that *Strand* was something of a life-changing record for me, and seeing the group play in New York City in the spring of 1996 was a seismic performance. The group was then in their duo iteration: Rebecca Gates on vocals and guitar, and Scott Plouf on drums. They were joined for much of their set by Elliott Smith on backing vocals, a role that he also played on *Strand*. At a time that I was most zeroed in on listening to predominantly straight-edge hardcore, it expanded my horizons considerably.

Twenty Minutes' Road

When I was growing up, there was a painting of mysterious origin hanging near the front door of my parents' house. I liked the idea of following one character over several decades, and the idea that they might become fixated on this work with a nebulous history seemed like a good fit for that. The idea of a work that inspires someone and turns out to be somewhat poisonous in its origins is also something that I explored in a drawer novel, the first third of which I periodically think about revisiting.

Spencer Hangs Over Newark

The version of the story that I first sent out for consideration for publication is what is now the story's first half. Todd Dills, editor of THE2NDHAND, accepted it, but suggested that I expand it, that Spencer's story wasn't yet complete. It took a little bit of time to get my head around this and figure out a way that I could continue things. Eventually, I went back to that perennial source of inspiration: Brian Eno. Eno's album Ambient 1: Music For Airports was a huge inspiration for the mood and the stillness of Spencer flying over the country. In order for a segment in which he would be in a much more focused motion, I settled on Talking Heads' *Remain in Light* as a touchstone, and went from there.

Stanton Sees, Stands, Stares

I was asked to contribute a story to *Hair Lit, Vol. 1*, an anthology featuring stories inspired by hair metal songs. (Fantastic writers like Roxane Gay, Lindsay Hunter, and Susannah Felts all have work in the book in question.) I ended up opting for Damn Yankees' "High Enough," a song that a younger version of me was, I'm reluctant to say, somewhat obsessed with in his early teenage years. Said younger version of me had a fairly massive sentimental streak, and was also blissfully unaware of Ted Nugent's extremely dodgy political beliefs.

The Independence Shipping Company

One of my earliest memories is taking a ferry with my parents. I'm not entirely sure where: I was very young at the time, and my mind has jumbled that memory up with one of visiting the New York Aquarium. While roundabout travels are something I'm very familiar with, the Staten Island Ferry doesn't run anywhere near Coney Island—so this one remains something of a mystery. When I was on a ferry headed to Nantucket late in 2012, the idea of a ferry as the setting of a story began to run through my head. By the time when, a little less than three years later, I was on a ferry from Seattle to Bremerton, the surreal world in which this story took place had begun to solidify. I jotted down some notes about the experience: the layout of the ship, the way that motion through the water felt, the places where one could observe the outside world. I had bittersweet thoughts on my mind in the writing of this one: a sense of progression, and the unquiet feelings that come when you realize that you're on a different course than some of your friends and peers.

The title is something of an homage to Robert Fripp and Brian Eno's "The Heavenly Music Corporation."

Some Things I Botched

I'm not sure where the central idea for this came from. I think it may have been born from a desire to experiment—to try writing something in very small increments. Slowly, they came together. Part of it was also being curious to work a bit with pronouns: the shift, briefly, from "I" to "we" and back again. (There's another story of mine, not collected in here, that's something of a descendent of this one, at least in this aspect.)

I wrote a lot of this in small sittings at a Starbucks near the Exchange Place PATH station in Jersey City. If my schedule at the job I was working at the time allowed for it, I'd spend fifteen or twenty minutes sitting there after the work day ended. I'd look across the Hudson at Lower Manhattan, I'd put my fingers on the keys, and I'd start to write.

Thanks to the following publications for publishing these stories:

Storychord ("Winter Montage, Hoboken Station"), Joyland ("The Wenceslas Men" and "An Old Songwriter's Trick"), Necessary Fiction ("Last Screening of A Hoax Cantata"), Midnight Breakfast ("Airport Hotel Ghost Tour"), 3:AM ("A Record Called 'American Woodworking'"), The Collapsar ("You In Reverse"), THE2ND-HAND ("Party Able Model," "Western Bridges," and "Spencer Hangs Over Newark"), Vol.1 Brooklyn ("Dulcimers Played, Strings Played"), Difficult Christmas ("Why I Was Not In New Jersey For Christmas In 1997"), Word Riot ("Twenty Minutes' Road"), Hair Lit, Vol.1 ("Stanton Sees, Stands, Stares"), and Everyday Genius ("Some Things I Botched").

Thanks as well to the editors and curators involved:

Sarah Lynn Knowles, Brian Joseph Davis, Emily Schultz, Alexander Houstoun, Rebecca Rubenstein, Taylor Pavlik, Nathan Knapp, James Brubaker, Nicholas Rombes, Pete Carvill, Todd Dills, Jeb Gleason-Allured, Jason Diamond, Ryan Sartor, Kevin Nguyen, Bryant Musgrove, Melissa Swantkowski, Jaime Green, Jackie Corley, Nick Ostdick, Penina Roth, and Dolan Morgan.

Thanks to the following people for making these stories, and this book, possible:

Michael J. Seidlinger, Sean H. Doyle, Jason Diamond, Scott Shields, Lauren Holt, Molly Templeton, Steve Shodin, Al and Angela Ming, Michele Filgate, Kristen and Charlie Marttila, Łukasz Janik, Maggie Flattery, Nicole Haroutunian, Alex Meyer, Anna Oler, Megan Kimball, Martin Olson, Jessie Schwartz, Jen Vafidis, Jenn Northington, Sarah McCarry, Mike Burmeister, Heather Muse, Jeremy and Sarah Olson, Stephanie Anderson, Trevor Ingerson, Jacqueline Mabey, Jordan Ginsberg, Theo Travers, Daphne Carr, and Mairead Case. This is in no way a complete list, but it's a start. Biggest of thanks go to my parents, Tom and Barbara Carroll, who from an early age set an example for me as readers, and whose encouragement throughout the years has been invaluable.

OFFICIAL

CCM ⬤

GET OUT OF JAIL
* VOUCHER *

- -

Tear this out.

Skip that social event.

It's okay.

You don't have to go if you don't want to. Pick up
the book you just bought. Open to the first page.
You'll thank us by the third paragraph.

If friends ask why you were a no-show, show them
this voucher.

You'll be fine.

- -

We're coping.

⬤

CPSIA information can be obtained at www.ICGtesting.com
Printed in the USA
BVOW08s1943170816

459357BV00002B/4/P